Jilly Cooper

Octavia

CORGI BOOKS

OCTAVIA
A CORGI BOOK : 0 552 10717 4

Originally published in Great Britain by
Arlington Books Ltd.

Arlington Books edition published 1977
Corgi edition published 1978
Corgi edition reprinted 1978
Corgi edition reprinted 1979 (twice)
Corgi edition reprinted 1980 (twice)
Corgi edition reprinted 1981
Corgi edition reprinted 1982
Corgi edition reprinted 1983
Corgi edition reprinted 1984
Corgi edition reprinted 1986
Corgi edition reprinted 1987
Corgi edition reissued 1989
Corgi edition reprinted 1989 (twice)
Corgi edition reprinted 1991
Corgi edition reprinted 1992
Corgi edition reprinted 1994
Corgi edition reissued 1996

Corgi Books are published by Transworld Publishers Ltd,
61–63 Uxbridge Road, London W5 5SA,
in Australia by Transworld Publishers (Australia) Pty Ltd,
15–25 Helles Avenue, Moorebank, NSW 2170,
and in New Zealand by Transworld Publishers (NZ) Ltd,
3 William Pickering Drive, Albany, Auckland.

Printed and bound in Great Britain by
Cox & Wyman Ltd, Reading, Berkshire

Jilly Cooper comes from Yorkshire but now lives in Gloucestershire with her family and an assortment of dogs and cats. Her journalism was a feature for many years of *The Sunday Times* and she has made many television appearances, including *What's My Line?* She has written six romances: *Emily, Bella, Harriet, Octavia, Prudence* and *Imogen.* Her novels, *Riders, Rivals, Polo* and *The Man Who Made Husbands Jealous* are also published by Corgi and were all Number One bestsellers. Her latest novel *Appassionata,* is now available as a Bantam Press hardback.

Also by Jilly Cooper

THE MAN WHO MADE HUSBANDS JEALOUS
POLO
RIVALS
RIDERS
EMILY
BELLA
HARRIET
PRUDENCE
IMOGEN
LISA & CO.

and published by Corgi Books

For Emma Renton
with Love

AUTHOR'S NOTE

The idea for OCTAVIA first came to me in 1968. I wrote it as a long short story called OCTOBER BRENNEN and it appeared in serial form in *Petticoat*. I then took the story and completely re-wrote it, and the result is
OCTAVIA.

I

The moment I set eyes on Jeremy West I knew I had to have him. I was sitting in Arabella's, watching a crowd of debs and other phonies undulating round the floor and thinking they were dancing, when suddenly the bamboo curtain was pushed aside and a blond man walked in and stood looking around for a waitress.

Even in the gloom with which Arabella's conceals its decor I could see that he had class—tall and lean, with one of those beautiful high cheek-boned faces with long, dreamy eyes like Rudolph Nureyev.

As the waitress came up to him, I watched to see if he'd leer down her exposed jacked-up bosom. He didn't. She led him to a table next but one to ours. He was obviously waiting for someone. Then a plump girl came through the bamboo curtains and stood blinking round with short-sighted eyes. He stood up and waved to her, and her face broke into a smile that was faintly familiar. Then I recognized her. It was Gussie Forbes; we'd been at school together. How on earth had she managed to land a havoc-maker like that?

'Look,' I said, nudging Charlie. 'That's Gussie Forbes, we were at school together.'

Charlie peered over his very dark glasses, which he only wears to emphasize his Mafia-like appearance.

'She doesn't seem to have recovered from it as well as you have,' he said. 'She obviously skips the features on slimming, when she reads women's magazines, and concentrates on the ones about "three dimensional charm". I suppose you want to rush over and reminisce about the "dorm" and the French mistress's beard?'

But I wasn't listening any longer.

'Do look,' I said. 'He's ordering champagne. Do you suppose they're celebrating?'

'Can't be much to celebrate, getting lumbered with a bird that looks like that,' said Charlie, beckoning the waitress and ordering more whisky.

Charlie is immensely successful, newly rich, young and, like me, rootless. He is not interested in anyone unless they're likely to advance his career or improve his image. At that time, just as I was getting bored with him, he was beginning to fall in love with me. This irked rather than worried me. I was used to men falling in love with me. When I gave Charlie the push, he would nurse his hurt pride for a fortnight, change the colour of his Ferrari and move on to the next affaire.

I couldn't take my eyes off the man who was buying champagne for Gussie Forbes. She was raising her glass to him now, and he was holding her hand and smiling at her. He had a beautiful smile, gentle and creasing his face in all the right places. Now he was running a hand down her cheek. It was really most mystifying.

Charlie was rabbiting on about the chic men's clothes shop he owns, who had been in, how difficult it was to get the right staff. Gussie and her man were getting up to dance. He moved easily, with the grace of some jungle cat. Gussie bounced around, wiggling her arms and her large bottom. She resembled a baby elephant taking a dip in the pool. Charlie took out a gold cigarette case, lit two cigarettes and handed one to me. He is full of these self-consciously sexy gestures which only work if you're Cary Grant.

Gussie was now writhing and pushing her hair about in utter abandon.

'They never taught your girlfriend to dance at school,' Charlie said, watching her in appalled amusement.

'She was taller than most of us then, so she always had to dance man.'

8

The floor had filled up now and Gussie and her man were dancing close together. He pressed his cheek against her hair, but his eyes wandered lazily around the room. Her eyes were closed in ecstasy and she had a fatuous smile on her face. God, she was just as wet as she had been at school!

Charlie put his hand on my thigh and drained his glass. 'Shall we go?' he said.

'In a minute. Let's have one more drink.'

The music had stopped, and they were coming off the floor right past our table. I ran my hand through my hair to loosen it and pulled the front piece over one eye.

'Hullo Gussie,' I said loudly.

'For God's sake,' whispered Charlie.

Gussie peered through the gloom, blinking.

'Over here,' I said.

Suddenly she saw me and gave a shriek of schoolgirl excitement.

'Goodness, it can't be, Octavia! Is it really you?'

'Yes, really me. Come and have a drink.'

Gussie pushed through the tables, pink face shining with excitement, bosom heaving from her exertions.

'How lovely to see you.' She kissed my proffered cheek. 'And looking so stunning too!'

She dragged the blond man forward. 'This is Jeremy West. It's a very special evening for us, we've just got engaged!'

Engaged! Hence the champagne. At least they weren't married yet!

'Congratulations,' I said, and gave Jeremy West one of my long, hard, smouldering looks. 'How very exciting.'

He smiled back at me. 'Yes, isn't it?'

'Jeremy darling,' said Gussie. 'This is Octavia Brennen. We were at school together, in the same form, but not for very long. Octavia did something perfectly dreadful like eating one of the harvest festival apples in church, so they sent her away. Life was very dull after that.'

'I can imagine it was,' said Jeremy West. Oh, how heart-breaking that smile was.

9

'This is Charles Mancini,' I said.

Charlie nodded enigmatically. With his Mexican bandit's face, pink suede suit and dark grey shirt, he looked both sinister and glamorous. No girl could be ashamed of being seen with Charlie.

'Why don't we all have a drink?' I said, ignoring a vicious kick on the ankles from Charlie.

Gussie looked up at Jeremy. 'Why not?' she said.

He nodded. 'Charlie, get the waitress to bring some more chairs,' I said.

'What were you drinking?' said Charlie sulkily.

'Champagne,' I said. 'It's a celebration.'

'I've had quite enough to drink, I'm already getting giggly,' said Gussie. 'Can I have some orange squash?'

I told you she was wet.

'But you'll have champagne?' Charlie said to Jeremy.

'I much prefer whisky. Let me buy this round.'

Charlie shook his head and summoned the waitress.

'You actually got engaged today?' I said.

'Well, yesterday,' said Gussie, hauling a bra strap up a fat white shoulder.

'Have you got a ring?'

'Yes. Isn't it lovely?' She held out a short stubby hand that had never seen a manicure in its life. On the third finger glowed an antique ring—rubies and pearls surrounded a plait of hair.

Of course he would choose something as subtly pretty as that. All the guys I knew would have given me solitaires or sapphires as big as a gull's egg.

'It's gorgeous,' I said looking through my hair at Jeremy. 'You are lucky, Gussie. Really beautiful men with exquisite taste into the bargain are at a premium these days.'

Charlie, busy ordering drinks, missed that remark. Jeremy blushed slightly.

'Yes, he is beautiful, isn't he,' sighed Gussie. 'I have to keep pinching myself to prove it's not a dream that he should have chosen an old frump like me.'

'When you've both finished discussing me like a prize

bull . . .' said Jeremy, but he said it gently and, taking a loose strand of Gussie's hair, smoothed it behind her ear.

The drinks arrived.

'Gosh, thanks awfully. It's terribly kind of you,' said Gussie, beaming at Charlie. I remembered of old how ridiculously grateful she'd always been about the smallest things.

'And that's a beautiful suit,' she added wistfully. 'Jeremy would look divine in clothes like that, but he's such an old square.'

I waited for Charlie to wince, but he didn't and was soon telling her all about the shop. That was another thing about her, she always managed to make people talk about themselves, and gave the impression she was really interested.

I gave Jeremy a long speculative look. He dropped his eyes first and took a gulp of whisky.

'That's better. I've never been wild about champagne.'

'I only like it for elevenses,' I said. 'When are you getting married?'

'November, we thought.'

'Not before! But that's light years away! Why on earth wait so long?'

'I've got a large overdraft already, and I don't relish the idea of living off Gussie.'

Gussie, I remembered, had a bit of money of her own.

'What do you do?'

'I'm in publishing, as an editor. I write a bit myself as well.'

'What sort of things?'

'Oh, poetry, a bit of criticism, the odd review, nothing likely to make any money.'

He looked like a poet with those dreamy blue eyes and long blond hair, yet it wasn't a weak face; there was a strength about the mouth and chin. I got out a cigarette; he lit it for me. I held his hand to steady the flame, looking up at him from under my lashes. Surely he could feel the electricity between us? He put away his lighter.

'Why are you called Octavia?'

'I was born on October the 25th. My mother'd gone off my

father by then and was mad about someone else, and she couldn't have been less amused by my arrival, or be bothered to think of a name for me. So she called me after the month. It's a damn silly name to be saddled with.'

'It's a beautiful name. It suits you. Did your mother marry the man she was mad about?'

'Oh no, someone quite different, and then someone else, and then someone else. My father was married twice too, but he's dead now. I've lost count of my stepbrothers and sisters.'

'It can't have been very easy for you. I come from a broken home myself, but not one that's in smithereens. Do you see your mother?'

'Occasionally, when she's sober, or comes to London. I hardly ever go down to the country to see her. I hate scenes. She's rather sad now. Her looks are going and she gets terrible maudlin fits reminiscing about my father, which drive her present husband mad.'

How gentle and compassionate his eyes were now, and how ridiculously long his eyelashes.

'I'm sorry,' I said, putting a husky little break into my voice that I'd perfected over the years. 'I didn't mean to bore you with family history. I never talk about it usually.'

That was a lie. It was Act I in the Octavia Brennen seduction routine—make them feel I need looking after.

'I'm flattered you told me,' he said.

'How did you two meet?'

'Gussie came and did temporary typing for me while my own secretary was skiing. She wasn't wildly efficient, every letter had to be typed over again, and she kept putting things in the wrong envelopes, but she was so sweet that when my own streamlined secretary came back and restored order, I realized I was missing Gus. I telephoned the agency, started taking her out and that was that.'

'I'm not surprised; she's so lovely.' I hoped he couldn't detect the whopping ring of insincerity in my voice. 'She always protected me from all the bullies when we were at school.'

'Yes, she grows on you.'

She was evidently growing on Charlie.

'Once I tried to diet faithfully,' she was saying. 'Day after day, week after week, not eating a thing but lettuce and steamed fish. But all I'd lost after six weeks was half an inch in height!' She shrieked with laughter. So did Charlie and Jeremy.

They were playing the Rolling Stones latest record. I leaned forward, pressing my elbows together to deepen my cleavage. I saw Jeremy glance down at it and quickly glance away.

'I'm mad for this tune,' I said.

'What are we waiting for?' said Charlie, getting up.

Dancing is the thing I do best in the world. It seems to release all the frustrations from my body, all the evils from my soul.

I was wearing a long, gold, semi-transparent tunic, exactly the same colour as my hair, with a mass of gold chains round my neck. I felt like a piece of seaweed streaming with the tide of the music, flowing now this way, now that. I knew everyone in the room was watching me, the women with envy, the men with lust.

Charlie dances superbly too; his body seems to turn to rubber. I never fancy him so much as when we're on the dance floor. Through a sheet of gold hair I saw Jeremy was watching me. He turned and said something to Gussie; she smiled and looked in my direction. The music stopped; hand-in-hand Charlie and I wandered back to our table.

'We're off,' I said, deciding this was the ideal exit note.

'Going home?' said Gussie.

'No, we're going to another place,' said Charlie. 'It's just been opened by a mate of mine. Want to come?' He *had* changed his tune.

Jeremy looked at Gussie; she shook her head.

'We've both got to get up early in the morning, but do give me your telephone number, Octavia. We must keep in touch.'

'We must,' I said, staring shamelessly at Jeremy. 'You must both come to dinner.'

'Yes, we'd like to,' he said, emphasizing the 'we'.

Even when we finally got home, I was still walking on air, unable to keep the Cheshire cat grin of exultation off my face. As the lift shot up to the penthouse flat I had the feeling it might take me through the roof straight up to the stars.

My flat was beautiful. Alexander, my brother, who is an expert at interior decorating, had helped me do it up. Everyone gasped when they first saw it. Huge fleshy potted plants, banked at each end of the long drawing room, gave the effect of a jungle. The fourth wall was all window, looking out onto the lamp-lit plane trees of Green Park. Kicking off my shoes, I felt my feet sink into the thick, white carpet.

Almost immediately the telephone rang.

'Answer it, would you?' I said to Charlie.

'Yeah?' said Charlie, picking up the receiver. 'It's someone called Ricardo,' he added. 'He sounds a long way away.'

'Crackling with lust,' I said, taking the receiver. 'Go and get a bottle out of the fridge, darling,' I said to him loudly, so Ricardo could hear.

'Hi, my darling,' I said to Ricardo.

When I had taken my time over the telephone call, I wandered into the bedroom. Charlie was lying naked on the blond fur counterpane, drinking champagne and looking beautiful and sulky. On the wall above his head hung my favourite picture: a 16th century Italian oil painting of Adam and Eve in the garden of Eden, surrounded by hundreds of animals and birds.

'It's vital,' my brother had insisted, 'to have something pretty to look at over one's bed to while away the excruciating boredom of sexual intercourse.' I knew that picture pretty well.

Ignoring Charlie, I undressed unhurriedly and sat down at my dressing table, admiring my reflection in the triple mirror. I liked what I saw. My body was as warm as an apricot in the soft light, my breasts, in contrast with the extreme slenderness of the rest of my body, had a heavy golden ripeness. Voluptuously I began to brush my hair.

'Who's Ricardo?' said Charlie, trying to appear cool.

'A rather persistent bit of my past,' I said. 'You know I never let a dago by.'

Charlie laughed. 'I hope he is past.'

He got up, crossed the room and stood behind me, his hands caressing my shoulders. His body was dark brown from the Marbella sun as he bent his head to kiss me. I could see the gold streaks growing out of his dark hair.

We made a stunning picture, like a Fellini film.

'Come on, Narcissus,' he said. 'It's time for bed.'

Afterwards he reached out for the champagne and gave me a glass.

'Christ, you were sensational tonight,' he muttered sleepily, as I examined my now tousled but not unpleasing reflection in the mirror opposite. 'What got into you?'

'You did,' I said, and laughed softly. There was no need to tell him the whole time we had been making love I had been practising every trick in the trade, imagining he was Jeremy West.

He fell asleep almost immediately, with his arms around me. It was terribly hot. I soon wriggled out of his embrace, and lay on my back, thinking about Jeremy, memorizing every angle of his face and every word he'd spoken to me. The fact that he was engaged to Gussie didn't worry me a bit, made it more of a challenge.

Eventually I got up, went to the bathroom, removed every scrap of make-up, then luxuriously massaged skin food all over my body. Then I took a couple of sleeping pills, switched off the telephone and fell into a dreamless sleep.

2

When I awoke at two o'clock in the afternoon Charlie had gone, leaving me a note on the pillow, saying he loved me, and to ring him when I was conscious. I switched on the telephone, it rang almost immediately. "Ullo, this is the Moroccan Embassy,' I said.

'Octavia, you *are* dreadful; it's Gussie here,' came the breathless, eager voice.

'Gussie, how lovely!'

'I thought I'd ring straightaway, before we lost touch.'

'You must come to dinner,' I said.

'We'd love to, but actually we've got a plan. Are you doing anything the weekend after next?'

'I'm supposed to be going to France, but it's a fluid arrangement.'

'Well, I expect you'd find it awfully boring, but Jeremy shares a boat with another chap, and we've got it next weekend. We wondered if you'd like to come too.'

'I might get seasick,' I said, trying to keep the excitement out of my voice.

'Oh you couldn't! It's a barge, and all we do is drift up and down the canals, going through the locks and tying up where it takes our fancy. Would you like to bring Charlie?'

'He'll be away,' I lied. 'It's not a big thing, Charlie and me, we're just mates.'

'You haven't got someone special you'd like to bring?'

'I did have. We were going to get married, but he was killed in a car crash earlier this year.'

'Oh, poor, poor Tavy,' she said, unconsciously lapsing into the nickname of schooldays. 'Oh God, I'm sorry.'

There was a pause.

'Well, anyway,' she floundered on. 'If you didn't want to

bring someone, Jeremy had thought . . . do you know Gareth Llewellyn?'

'No, should I? The name sounds faintly familiar.'

'He's a great friend of Jeremy's. We've been trying to persuade him to come on the boat for ages, but he works so hard, he can never get away. I think you'd like him; he's awfully attractive.'

I didn't care if he were. My mind was already jumping ahead, dreaming of a long weekend, drifting up and down the canals, lounging on the deck in my bikini by day, my hair gleaming pale in the moonlight by night—how could I not hook Jeremy?

'It sounds great,' I said. 'I'd love to come. Why don't you and Jeremy come to dinner on Monday and we can talk about it?'

I planned Monday's dinner like a military operation. As I'm a rotten cook and can be guaranteed to louse up even fake mashed potato, I arranged for the food to be sent up from the restaurant around the corner, so I could pass it off as my own efforts.

Gussie had obviously given Jeremy the impression that I was a frivolous social butterfly and I was determined to dispel it. I scoured the shops until I found a dress that made me look both demure and sexy, and I bought all Jeremy's books—two slender volumes of poetry and a book of criticism of John Donne's poems. I found Jeremy's poems quite incomprehensible. The long, rather self-admiring introduction written by Jeremy himself made me understand them even less.

The doorbell rang as I was spraying scent round the flat. Gussie stood in front of Jeremy, clutching a huge box of chocolates.

'For you,' she said, giving me a bear hug. 'You're the only friend I have who doesn't need to diet. Goodness, that blue looks stunning!'

I couldn't say the same for her. She was wearing a scarlet dress which clashed horribly with her flushed face. We went

17

into the drawing-room and I poured everyone stiff drinks.

'How delicious to have a flat like this all to oneself,' said Gussie, collapsing on to the sofa.

'I can't wait to get out of London on Friday,' I said.

'Nor can I,' said Gussie, shovelling nuts into her face like a starved squirrel. 'My office is like a furnace. Gareth *is* coming, by the way. I lured him by telling him what a knockout you were.'

'Well then, he's doomed to bitter disappointment,' I said with a sidelong glance at Jeremy.

'Not in your case,' he said, staring back at me until I demurely dropped my eyes.

Oh Good-ee, I thought, it's beginning to work. I sat on the sofa, stretching long brown legs in front of me. I saw Jeremy looking at them surreptitiously. I didn't blame him, they were a far prettier sight than Gussie's tree trunks, displayed almost in their entirety by a rucked-up skirt.

'Gareth wants us to go round after dinner for a drink,' she said. 'He says he can't wait until Friday.'

'Do you like him?' I asked Jeremy, as though it were only his opinion that mattered.

'Yes, I do. He's one of my oldest friends. We were at Oxford together. His father was a Welsh miner, and he was a scholarship boy with a chip as big as a plank on his shoulder. Then he ended up with a first.'

'He's got a mind like a steel trap but he's not at all academic,' added Gussie. 'All he's ever wanted to do is make masses of money. He's got his own company now, with thousands of little men working for him putting up sky-scrapers. He's the most energetic man I've ever met.'

'He sounds exhausting,' I said, filling Jeremy's drink.

'Not really,' said Jeremy. 'You occasionally feel you want to add water, but on the whole he's fine.'

'Won't he get bored on the boat?'

'Not with you around. He loves girls.'

'He has time for them?'

'Oh, yes,' sighed Gussie. 'He's awfully attractive. He makes you feel all body, somehow.'

Dinner was a success. Luigi's had surpassed themselves. Both Jeremy and Gussie were extremely impressed.

Over coffee, I opened Gussie's chocolates.

'Oh, we oughtn't to,' said Gussie, rootling round for a soft centre. 'We bought them for you.'

It was then that I played my trump card. Turning to Jeremy I said, 'You never let on you were *the* Jeremy West. You've been a god of mine ever since I can remember. I've got all your books.'

How sweet he looked when he blushed.

'And you've actually read them?'

'Of course. I know most of your poems by heart. I like the one about Victoria Station late at night best.' I reeled off a few lines.

After that nothing stopped him. The occasional murmur from me was all he needed. I didn't listen to what he was saying, I was too busy gazing hypnotically into his eyes. It was Gussie who finally halted him, when she'd finished the chocolates.

'Dar-ling, if we're going to Gareth's, it's gone ten o'clock.'

He was all contrition. 'Sweetheart, I *am* sorry. When I get on my hobby horse, it's like crossing a motorway in the rush-hour, trying to stop me.' He took her hand. 'It's so rare meeting someone who actually understands what I'm trying to say.'

'Unlike me,' said Gussie, without rancour. 'Let's quickly do the washing-up.'

'Absolutely not,' I said firmly. I wasn't going to have her finding Luigi's take-away carrier bags in the kitchen.

'Oh, well, if you insist. Can I go to the loo?'

Jeremy and I went into the drawing-room.

'There you are,' I said, pointing to his books on one of the bottom shelves. I'd taken the jackets off and dirtied them up a bit.

He looked at me for a second. 'You're very unexpected, you know.'

'I am?'

'Yeah. When we met last week I thought you were one of those impossibly beautiful girls, incapable of doing anything but look glamorous. Now I find you know how to make a flat look wonderful, you cook like an angel, and you seem to know more about books than any woman I've ever met!'

'I aim to please,' I said. 'Have you got a cigarette?'

'Of course.' He lit one for me.

'Gussie seems determined to get me off with this Gareth man.'

'Gussie's a romantic; she longs for everyone to be as happy as she is. I'm sure you'll like him. Most women do.'

'I'm choosy,' I said carefully. 'I prefer to do my own hunting.'

For the first time we really looked at each other, slowly, lingeringly, exploring each other's faces, unable to tear our eyes away.

'Stop it,' he said, but quite gently. 'Gussie'll be back in a minute.'

The hot June night blazed with stars. We drove through London with the roof down and the wireless blaring, in wild spirits. We were all a bit tight. As it was only a two-seater I had insisted on sitting in the luggage compartment on the right side so I could catch Jeremy's eye in the driving mirror. When we swung round corners I let my fingers rest lightly on his shoulder.

Suddenly I felt a pang. Perhaps it was a bit much trying to nick him from Gussie. Then I saw Gussie put her hand on his thigh, not in a very sexy way, just in a friendly gesture of togetherness, and I was shot through with jealousy. The pang disappeared. Any girl who let herself get as fat as Gussie deserved to lose a man like Jeremy anyway.

I managed to show as much leg as possible as I got out of the car. In the row of large white, elegant Kensington houses, Gareth Llewellyn's stood out like a sore thumb. It was painted violet, with a brilliant scarlet door. How ostentatious can you get, I thought.

Unexpectedly, the door was answered by a girl with long red hair, eyes the colour of greengages and endless legs.

'Mr. West,' she said, giving Jeremy a pussy-cat smile. 'Come in. Mr. Llewellyn is upstairs; perhaps you'd follow me.'

On the third floor, standing in the doorway, stood a tall, thickset man, smoking a cigar. Jeremy collapsed into his arms, clutching at his shirt and gasping out some story about having become separated from the main party with which he had scaled all but the final peak. 'Brandy,' he croaked and, staggering past the man with the cigar, collapsed onto a pile of cushions. Gussie shrieked with laughter.

'I think he's a bit tight. Hullo Gareth darling,' she said, kissing him. 'This is Octavia Brennen. Isn't she a knockout?'

'How do you do?' I said, putting on my society voice because I was embarrassed.

'Very well, thank you,' he mimicked me, looking me over very slowly, like a judge examining a show hack.

He turned and smiled at Gussie. 'She's beautiful, Gus. For once you haven't exaggerated.'

'Are you sure you two haven't met before?' said Gussie. 'I should have thought you would have, being jet-setters and all that.'

Gareth Llewellyn examined me a bit more and shook his head.

'No, I never forget a body. Did she really come up the stairs? I thought girls like that only came down the chimney at Christmas time.'

His voice was low in both senses of the word, with a soft but very discernable Welsh accent. I had the feeling he was laughing at me. Gussie shrieked with more giggles; she was beginning to get seriously on my nerves.

We joined Jeremy in a room which looked like the sunset people walk hand-in-hand into, at the end of technicolor films —brilliant pink walls, covered in books and paintings, scarlet curtains, parquet glimmering in pools round flamingo-coloured longhaired rugs, piles of white fur cushions and a long orange sofa. It was vulgar, but it worked. Papers were scattered over the floor and the girl who'd let us in started picking them up.

'I love your cushions,' said Gussie, collapsing onto a pile beside Jeremy.

'I took my hangover to Habitat last Saturday and bought them. At least they keep everyone horizontal,' said Gareth, winking at me and moving towards a bookshelf of leather-bound volumes. The next moment he'd pressed a button and the entire works of Walter Scott slid back to reveal a vast cocktail cabinet.

'Now,' he said. 'What would anyone like?'

He was absolutely *not* my type. His face was heavy with a powerful butt of a jaw, big crooked nose, full sensual mouth and wicked black eyes which seemed to be continually laughing at some private joke.

His skin was swarthy, and his thick black hair, prematurely streaked with grey, grew over his collar and in long sideboards down his cheeks. He was wearing light grey corduroy trousers and a dark blue shirt, open at the neck to show a mat of black hair. His height and massive shoulders didn't entirely draw the eye away from a thickening waistline.

He handed me a drink. 'There you are, baby. It's a real L.O.'

'L.O.?'

'Leg opener. Never fails to work.'

Blushing angrily, I turned away.

By the time he had fixed us all drinks, the beautiful red-head had collected all the papers from the floor.

'You haven't met my P.A., Mrs. Smith, have you?' said. Gareth. 'Now, in her case the 'A' stands for Aphrodisiac. Do you want a drink, lovely?'

She shook her head and gave him her pussy-cat smile.

'I ought to be getting home. My poor husband will be wondering what the hell's happened.'

'I'll see you out,' said Gareth. 'I won't be a minute,' he added to us.

'Isn't he gorgeous?' said Gussie.

'Great,' I replied, unenthusiastically.

There was a crude power about him. I could see why certain women might go for him—but not me. I detest those big, hunky aggressively sexual men; they make me feel claustrophobic. I like my men gentle, reticent, subtle. Gareth Llewellyn was about as subtle as a steam roller in overdrive.

I wandered round the room examining objects and giving Jeremy the opportunity to admire my figure. I avoided looking into an adjoining room, after glimpsing one of the biggest double beds I'd ever seen. I half expected to see a blond in gold lame pyjamas revving-up beneath the sheets.

A slight breeze swayed the curtains, bringing a scent of mignonette and tobacco plants from the window box outside. I looked out of the window. Down below Gareth Llewellyn was talking to Mrs. Smith. Suddenly he pulled her into his arms and kissed her very thoroughly. After a minute, he let her go and opened the car door for her. She patted his cheek with her hand.

As he turned to come back into the house, he looked up and caught me looking at him, and grinned.

The telephone rang. Gussie picked up the receiver.

'Hullo, yes. He's downstairs. Hang on a minute. Gareth,' she yelled, 'telephone.'

He grimaced apologetically at us as he came in and took the receiver.

'Vinnie, baby, how are you? Yeah. I've missed you too. Sweetheart, I haven't a hope this evening. I'm knee-deep in people, and later I've got to work. I've got one hell of a day tomorrow. Listen, darling, what about Wednesday evening?' God, that Welsh voice could turn it on.

Trying not to listen, I turned to Jeremy. He smiled at me reassuringly.

'What other writers do you like?' I said.

'Keats, of course, Thomas Campion, some of A. E. Housman.'

'What do you think of Robert Browning?' I asked.

'Why?' said Gareth, coming off the telephone. 'Is he marry-

23

ing anyone we know?'

Gussie giggled. 'You mustn't mob them up; they've been having high-powered intellectual conversations all evening. Don't you think, Tavy, that the colours of Gareth's curtains would be ideal for my bridesmaids?'

After that I was forced to listen to her rabbiting on about her wedding. I lounged on the floor, propped against the sofa, lacing my fingers behind my head to show off my bust, and rucking up my skirt. With my other ear, I listened to Jeremy's conversation with Gareth.

'Is that bird really your secretary?'

'Mrs. Smith?' said Gareth. 'Quite a doll isn't she?'

'Doesn't she mind working at this hour?'

'Mr. Smith is an in-work actor; irregular hours suit her. So stop eating your heart out, you'll never get your spoon into that pudding.'

The telephone rang. It was South America on the line. Gareth, claiming it was business, took it into the bedroom. Jeremy and I helped ourselves to more drink.

'Does he always carry on like this?' I said.

'With girls? Usually, not always. He isn't trying to prove anything, he's just a glutton. He can't pass anyone up.'

'He ought to get married,' said Gussie. 'He needs the love of a good woman.'

'He'd need the love of four good mistresses as well to keep him going,' I said. 'Are you installing a telephone on the boat?'

'No, that's one of the conditions of his coming down, no telephones,' said Gussie. 'I'm going to make some coffee.'

She wandered out of the room. I got to my feet and strolled over to the fireplace to examine the pile of invitations—parties, dinners, business functions. Jeremy came over and stood beside me. I looked up at our reflections side by side in the huge mirror above the fireplace.

'How odd,' I said slowly. 'Have you noticed how alike we are, both blue-eyed and blonde? We could be brother and sister. I've always felt incest has the edge on all other relationships.'

Jeremy's breath was coming rapidly and his eyes had gone

almost glazed with lust.

'You must know I don't feel remotely brotherly towards you.'

I looked up at him, running my tongue slowly along my bottom lip.

'How *do* you feel?' I said softly.

'Bloody disturbed—and I'm not amused by sleepless nights either.'

'Oh, nor am I, nor am I. We can't do anything about it, you know.'

'Of course we can't, but that doesn't stop me being obsessed with you. You're the most beautiful girl I've seen in my life.' He paused. 'I suppose lots of men have told you that.'

'A few. Not many of them meant it.'

'Well I do,' he said angrily.

'Do you *not* want me to come on the boat?'

'Of course I want you to . . . and, well . . . Gussie would be so disappointed.'

'You realize how difficult it's going to be, being thrown together all the time.'

'We shall probably both go mad, but rather that than you staying away because of me.'

I took a step towards him. 'We shall both have to rely on self-control, that's all.'

'Oh, I shouldn't do that,' said a voice from the doorway. 'It's not infallible in my experience . . .'

We spun around, appalled to find Gareth watching us. His eyes weren't laughing now. There was a calm, bland, dangerous look about him, but all he said was, 'Your glass is empty, Octavia.'

Then Gussie came bustling in with the coffee. How much had he heard? I bit my lip with vexation.

After that we talked about plans for the weekend, who should bring what, what route we should take. I didn't contribute much. I was too shattered. I couldn't look at Jeremy.

'When are you planning to drive down?' Gareth asked.

'Lunchtime on Friday. And you?'

'I've got meetings all day. I won't be able to make it much before five.' He turned to me. 'When do you knock off work?'

'I don't work,' I said haughtily.

'No, I should have realized that. Your private life must be a full-time activity. I'll give you a lift down.'

'No,' I said, much too quickly. 'I want to go down early with Jeremy and Gussie; then I can help them get the boat cleaned up.'

Suddenly his swarthy face was a mask of malice. 'Don't you think the young lovers should have some time on their own? Three's a crowd and all that.'

'Yes, you go with Gareth, Tavy,' said Gussie, pleased that her match-making was working out. 'It'll be nice for him to have someone to drive down with. It's a rough old job getting the boat ready, but it'll be all beautiful by the time you both arrive.'

'I'm not afraid of hard work,' I snapped.

'No, of course you're not,' she said soothingly. 'You can do the cooking on board, if it makes you any happier.'

It didn't. There wouldn't be any Luigi's restaurant to take food away from, on the backwaters of the Thames. I started to yawn.

'Octavia's tired,' said Jeremy. 'We must go.'

As we were going down the stairs, the telephone rang again. Gareth took it on the first floor.

'Charlotte, darling, great to hear you. Hang on love, I'm just seeing some people out.' He put his hand over the receiver. 'I'll see you all on Friday.' He turned to me. 'What's your address?'

'Eleven Mayfair Street.'

'I'll collect you about half-past five.'

'Isn't he a scream?' said Gussie, as we went out into the street.

'Oh blast, I've forgotten that list of houses he gave me.'

She charged back into the house.

Jeremy and I looked at each other. His eyes showed as two black patches in the pallor of his face.

'Do you think Gareth caught the gist of what we were

saying?' I said.

'I expect so. Doesn't matter. Did you fancy him after all that?'

'He's not my type. He looks like a lorry driver.'

'What is your type?'

'You are,' I said.

3

Next day the weather soared into the eighties. London wilted, but I blossomed. I felt absurdly and joyously happy, and spent most of the day lying naked on my balcony, turning brown and gazing up at a sky so blue that it reminded me of Jeremy's eyes.

I refused to go out with anyone that week, and made sure of ten hours' sleep every night by taking too many sleeping pills. I spent a fortune on clothes for the weekend. I was only faintly disappointed Jeremy didn't ring me. But I was ex-directory and he could hardly have got the number from Gussie.

On Thursday morning I had my recurrent nightmare—more terrifyingly than ever before. The dream always started the same way; my father was alive still, and although I was grown-up, I was paralysed with childish fears of the dark, creeping down the stairs, hearing the sound of my parents' quarrelling getting louder and louder, not daring to turn on the light because I knew my mother would shout at me. As I reached the bottom of the stairs, I could distinguish what my mother was saying in a voice slurred with drink.

'I've had enough, I'm leaving you, and I'm taking Xander with me.'

Then my father started shouting back that she'd take Xander over his dead body. Then my mother screaming, 'Well you can keep Octavia then.' And my father saying, 'I don't want Octavia. Why the bloody hell should anyone want Octavia when you've completely ruined her?'

'Someone's got to have her,' yelled my mother.

'Well, it's not going to be me.'

Then I started to scream, pushed open the door, and there was my mother, her beauty all gone, because she was drunk and red in the face. She and my father were both looking at me in guilt and horror, wondering how much of the conversation I'd heard. Then suddenly my father turned into Jeremy, shouting, 'I don't care how much she heard, I still don't want her.'

I woke up screaming my head off, the sheets were drenched with sweat. For a few minutes I lay with my eyes open, gulping with relief, listening to the diminishing drumbeats of my heart, feeling the horror receding. Then I got up, took a couple of Valium and lit a cigarette with a shaking hand. I had to talk to someone, just to prove that someone wanted me. If only I could ring Jeremy, but it was too early in the relationship to show him how vulnerable I was. Nor could I talk to Charlie. It would only start the whole thing up again. I caught sight of the silver framed photograph on the dressing table and realized with relief that Xander must be back from Bangkok. At that time Xander was the only person in the world I really loved and trusted; not that I trusted him to behave himself or not do the most disgraceful things, but because I knew he loved me and that that love was intensified by guilt because he realized our parents had adored him and never loved me. Xander, four years older than me, had always fought my battles in the nursery. He had protected me from the succession of nannies that my mother never got on with, and later from the succession of potential and actual stepfathers who thundered through the house.

I looked at my watch; it was 10.45. Even Xander—not famous for getting to the office on time—might just be in. I dialled Seaford-Brennen's number.

'Can I speak to Alexander Brennen please?'

Xander's secretary was a dragon, trained to keep the multitudes at bay, but she always put me through. Xander answered.

'Octavia darling, I was going to ring you today,' he said, in the light, flat drawling voice, which I always liked to think became gentler and less defensive when he talked to me.

'How was Bangkok?' I asked.

'Like a fairy tale—literally—I stayed in Pat Pong Street which was nothing but gay bars and massage parlours.'

I giggled.

'Do you want something?' said Xander, 'or are you just lonely?'

'I wanted a chat,' I said.

'A chap?'

'No, silly, just to talk to you.'

'Listen, I don't want to be unfriendly darling, but I'm a bit tied up at the moment. I've just got in and several people are trying to hold a meeting in my office. What are you doing for lunch?'

'Nothing.'

'O.K., I'll meet you at Freddy's at one o'clock.'

I lay back feeling better; the Valium were beginning to work. Soon I should feel strong enough to get down to the daily pastime of washing my hair.

Because of my grandfather, Henry Brennen, I didn't have to work for a living. After the First World War he came out of a fashionable regiment and, realizing he had no money left to support a wife and three children, the eldest of which was my father, joined forces with a fellow officer, William Seaford, to form a company, Seaford-Brennen, in the unfashionable field of electrical engineering. Both men were tough, astute and ambitious, and by dint of hard work and good luck, soon had factories turning out transformers, switchgear, generators and electric motors. Business prospered and survived the next war. After that, two rival heirs apparent joined the company—my father, who'd covered himself in glory as a Battle of Britain pilot, and William Seaford's far less dashing son Ricky, who'd spent most of the war in a routine staff job. My father had the additional kudos of having a new and ravishingly beautiful actress wife who promptly gave up work and produced a Brennen heir, while poor Ricky Seaford married a plain, domineering Yorkshire girl who, despite her capabilities on local committees and the golf course, only provided him with daughters.

My father, however, while appearing to hold all the cards, found it extremely difficult to settle down to a nine-to-five job after the excitement of the war. His restlessness increased as the years passed, and he discovered that my mother—who found him far less glamorous out of uniform—had started drinking too much, and launched herself on a succession of very indiscreet affairs.

By the time I was born in 1950, the marriage was well into injury time and my father even expressed grave doubts that I was his child which, I used to fantasise, explained his indifference to me. Despite such setbacks, he and my mother staggered on together for another six years, by which time old Henry Brennen had died of a heart attack and William Seaford had retired, having made his pile, leaving my father as chairman and Ricky as managing director. Ricky, meanwhile, the tortoise to my father's hare, had put his head down and spent the postwar years building up Seaford International, a vast empire of which Seaford–Brennen soon became only a subsidiary.

In 1956, my mother left home with my brother Xander and one of her lovers. A few months later she had a pang of guilt and sent for me and the nanny to live with her in France. My father was disconsolate for a short time, then moved in with his secretary whom he married as soon as he could divorce my mother. The marriage was extremely happy, and enabled my father to concentrate on work, and when he died, very young, of throat cancer, in 1971, he was able to leave huge blocks of Seaford–Brennen shares to Xander and me, which should have guaranteed us private incomes for life.

Alas, no income would have been enough for my brother Xander. Sacked from school for smoking grass and seducing too many new boys, he was also sent down from Cambridge after two terms for riotous living. Being artistically inclined, he would have been happier editing an art magazine or working in a gallery, but as the only existing Seaford–Brennen heir, he automatically went into the family firm. Here he survived— after my father was no longer alive to protect him—by the skin of his beautifully capped teeth, and by his immense personal charm. Three years ago, when Ricky Seaford was on the brink of sacking him, Xander redeemed himself by selling an Arab a power station worth millions of pounds in a deal carried out across the roulette table. Eighteen months later when things had again looked really dicey, Xander had played his trump card by running off with Ricky's elder daughter, Pamela, to the horror of both her parents. Even Ricky, however, didn't want to have the reputation in the city as the man who'd booted out his son-in-law. Xander was made export sales manager, which gave him access to vast expenses.

In his new, exalted position Xander had managed to fiddle the renting and re-decorating of my flat on the firm. After all, he said, one must have somewhere nice to take overseas clients. The firm also paid my rates, telephone, electricity and gas, and provided me with a car which I'd just smashed up. On the whole Xander and I did pretty well out of Seaford–Brennen.

While I was waiting for the conditioner to soak into my hair, I flipped through my wardrobe deciding what to take on the weekend. I'd bought so many new clothes this week, my cheque book had run out, but after the nasty letter I'd got from my bank manager, I didn't dare order another one. American Express and Access had also cut off their supplies. I still had to get another bikini and a glamorous dress to float around on deck. I'd have to borrow from Xander.

The doorbell rang. I peered through the spy hole looking out for creditors or unwelcome suitors, but all I could see were flowers. They turned out to be a huge bunch of pink roses in a plastic vase, filled with green spongy stuff, into which was stuck a mauve bow on a hatpin. I hoped for a blissful moment they were from Jeremy and felt a ridiculous thud of disappointment when the note in loopy florist's handwriting said: 'Don't cut me out of your life altogether, all love, Charlie.'

Charlie, I reflected as I rinsed and re-rinsed, was going to be as hard to get out of my hair as conditioner. I wondered how the hell I was going to survive the next 30-odd hours until I saw Jeremy again. I felt a restlessness like milk coming up to the boil, an excitement sometimes pleasurable, but far more often, painful.

4

The heatwave had set in relentlessly. The traffic glittered and flashed in the sunshine as it crawled up Piccadilly. The park was full of typists in bikinis, sliding off the deckchairs as the park attendant approached with his ticket machine. I could feel the tarmac burning through the soles of my shoes as I crossed the road to Freddy's. I nipped into the ladies first to tidy my hair and take the shine off my nose. I was wearing new pale pink dungarees with nothing underneath. I toyed with the idea of wearing them when I travelled down with Gareth tomorrow.

'Thank you very much,' I said in a loud voice to the cloakroom attendant as I left, just to draw her attention to the fact I'd put 50p in the saucer. Since I'd met Jeremy, sheer happiness made me overtip everyone.

Freddy's was packed as usual and giving off the same mydear-punctuated roar as a smart wedding. Along the bar sat advertising executives with brushed forward hair and romantic looking young men wearing open-necked shirts. Chatting them up were beautiful girls, their streaked hair swinging, their blusher in exactly the right place, their upper lips painted a perfect crimson double circumflex. As they sat, fingers tapping on their slim thighs, eyes flickering over each other's shoulders to see who had just come in, they constantly checked their appearance in the mirror above the bar. Freddy's was the current favourite haunt of trendies and showbusiness people, anyone in fact who was important enough to get in, and rich enough to get out.

Freddy, a mountain of a man with a face as red as a dutch cheese, was serving behind the bar.

'Hullo, ugly mug,' he bawled at me. 'How the hell did you get past the doorman?' Nearby drinkers looked at me in admiration. Only favourites and the famous got insulted. Freddy leaned over and pumped my hand vigorously.

'Where the hell you been anyway, Octavia? Sneaking over to Arabella's, I suppose. Can't say I blame you, I eat there too. The prices here are too high for me.' He bellowed with laughter, then added, 'Your no-good brother's already at the table upstairs drinking himself stupid.'

I followed the smell of garlic, wine and herbs up to the dining-room, waited in the doorway until I had everyone's undivided attention, then sauntered across the room. The pink dungarees definitely had the desired effect; the front flap only just covered my nipples.

Xander was sitting at a window table, flipping through a Sotheby's catalogue. He looked up, smiled, and kissed me on both cheeks. 'Hullo, angel, you look positively radiant. Have I forgotten your birthday or something?'

Waiters immediately rushed up, spreading a napkin across my knees, pushing in my chair, getting a waiting bottle of Poully Fuissé out of an ice bucket, and filling up my glass. Xander ordered another large whisky.

Perhaps it's because he *is* my brother that I always think Xander is the best looking man in the world. He is slim and immensely elegant, with very pale patrician features, brilliant

33

grey eyes, fringed by long dark lashes, and light brown hair, the colour mine was before I started bleaching it. Even on the hottest day of the year he gives the impression of a saluki shivering with overbreeding. As usual he was exquisitely dressed in a pale grey suit, grey and white striped shirt, and a pink tie.

Impossibly spoilt, with all the restlessness that comes with inherited wealth, he moved through life like a prince, expecting everyone to do exactly what he wanted, and capable of making himself extremely disagreeable if they did not. Few people realized how insecure he was underneath, or that he employed a technique of relentless bitching to cover up his increasing black glooms. He was always sweet to me, but I was very glad he was my brother and not a boyfriend. Part of his charm was that he always gave one his undivided attention. He didn't need to look over your shoulder, because he was always the one person people were looking over other people's shoulders to see.

On closer examination that day, he looked rather ill, his eyes laced with red, his hands shaking. He had placed himself with his back to the window, but still looked much younger than his thirty years.

'How are you?' I said.

'A bit poorly. I ran into a bottle of whisky last night. Later I landed up at Jamie Bennett's. We smoked a lot of grass. I'm sure it had gone off. There was a case of stuffed birds in the corner and Jamie started cackling with laughter, saying they were flying all over the room, then suddenly he was sick in a watepaper basket.'

'What happened to you?'

'I started feeling frightful too, and decided I must get home, so I drove very slowly to Paddington, but it wasn't there, so I came back again.'

I giggled. 'So you never got home?'

He shot me a sideways glance. 'Can I tell Pamela I spent last night at your place?'

'Of course,' I said lightly. 'It's only another point she'll notch up against me.'

Pamela had never forgiven me for slashing my wrists the day she and Xander got married, taking all the attention from her.

'How's our dear mother?' I said.

'Absolutely awful! You've no idea how lucky you are not being the apple of her eye. She rings up every day. Gerald is evidently threatening to walk out if she doesn't stop drinking, so she has to restort to having quick swigs in the lavatory.'

'Does she ever say anything about me?' I asked. Even now I can't mention my mother's name without my throat going dry.

'Never,' said Xander. 'Do you want to order?'

I wasn't hungry, but I hadn't eaten since yesterday lunchtime, and the wine was beginning to make me feel dizzy.

'I'll have a Cobb salad and a grilled sole,' I said.

'You really do look marvellous,' said Xander. 'What's up? Someone must be. Who's he married to?'

'No one,' I said, grooving four lines on the table cloth with my fork.

'There must be some complication.'

'He's engaged,' I said.

'I didn't know anyone did that any more. Who to?'

'An eager overgrown schoolgirl; she's so fat, wherever you stand in the room she's beside you.'

'Unforgiveable,' said Xander with a shudder. 'What's he like?'

'Tall and blond—almost as beautiful as you, and so gentle and sympatico.'

'Rich?'

'I don't know. I haven't asked him; not particularly.'

'Well that's no good then.' Xander broke a roll impatiently with his fingers, then left it. He watched his figure like a lynx. Then he sighed, 'You'd better tell me about him.'

Conversation was then impossibly punctuated by waiters laying tables, asking who was having the smoked trout, giving us our first courses, brandishing great phallic pepper pots over our plates, and pouring us more wine. A quarter of an hour later I was still picking bits of bacon out of my avocado and chopped spinach.

'Am I boring you?' I said.

'Yes,' said Xander gently. 'But it really doesn't matter. You have got him bad. What about Charlie?'

'Charlie who?' I said.

'Like that, is it? Who's going to be the other guy on the boat?'

'A friend of Jeremy's called Gareth Llewellyn.'

Xander looked up. 'He's supposed to be rather agreeable.'

'If you like jumped-up Welsh gorillas,' I said.

Xander laughed. 'He's phenomenally successful—and with birds too, one hears.'

'Oh, he's convinced he's got the master key to everyone's chastity belt,' I said. 'But I've had the lock changed on mine. He doesn't like me very much. He caught me swapping extravagant pleasantries with Jeremy. He knows something's up.'

'Well, I'd get him on my side, if I were you,' said Xander. 'He sounds pretty formidable opposition.'

Now we were into the rat-race of the second course. Waiters kept butting in, asking if I wanted my sole on or off the bone, offering vegetables and salads, more wine and more phallic pepper and tartare sauce.

'Everything all right, sir?' said the head waiter, hovering over us a minute later.

'Yes, perfect, if you'd go away and leave us alone,' snapped Xander.

'There's only one thing,' I said, pleating the table cloth with my fingers. 'Can you possibly lend me £200?'

'What for?' said Xander.

'I need some clothes for the weekend.'

'You've got quite enough,' sighed Xander. 'As it is, Covent Garden comes to you every time they want to dress an opera.'

'Just £200,' I pleaded. 'I promise, once I hook Jeremy I won't ask you for another penny.'

'Darling, you don't seem to realize that things are frightfully tight at the moment. There's a little thing called inflation which neither you nor Pamela seem to have heard of. We're all going to have to pull our horns in. My dear father-in-law's been on the warpath all morning, bellyaching about my expenses. I gather this year's accounts are pretty disastrous too.'

'For the whole group or just Seaford–Brennen?'

'Well Seaford–Brennen in particular. Everyone's very twitchy at the moment. Something's obviously up! Directors going round after dark piecing together one's torn-up memos. Every time you go down the passage, you're subjected to a party political broadcast on behalf of the accounts department. Both Glasgow and Coventry look as though they're going to come out on strike—the shop stewards so much enjoyed appearing on television last time.'

'Things'll get better,' I said, soothingly.

'Bloody well hope so,' said Xander. 'I've borrowed so much money from the company they'll have to give me a rise so I can pay them back. Thank God for Massingham, at least he's on my side.'

Hugh Massingham was managing director of Seaford–Brennen, a handsome, hard-drinking Northerner in his late forties, who liked Xander's sense of humour. They used to go on the tiles together, and bitch about Ricky Seaford. Hugh Massingham liked me too. When my father died six years ago he had looked after me, and eventually we'd ended up in bed. The affair had cooled down but we'd remained friends, and he still spent odd nights with me.

'He sent his love,' said Xander. 'Said he was going to come and see you next week.'

I wondered, now I'd fallen for Jeremy, if I'd be able to come up with the goods for Massingham any more. Never mind, I'd cross that bridge party when I came to it.

Depression suddenly seemed to encompass the table. I could feel one of Xander's black glooms coming on, probably caused by my tactlessly rabbiting on about Jeremy—which must only emphasize the stupid mockery of his marriage.

I took his hand.

'How's Pamela?' I said.

'Not awfully sunny at the moment. She's spending the

weekend at Grayston with Ricky and Joan, and I've refused to go. I have to put up with my dear father-in-law five days a week, I need a break at weekends. And I can put up with Joan even less, the great screeching cow. No one can accuse me of marrying Pamela for her Mummy.'

I giggled. 'What's she done now?'

'Alison's pregnant.'

'Oh God, I'm sorry.'

Alison was Pamela's younger sister, only married this year.

'And dear Joan never stops subtly rubbing Pammie's nose in it that she isn't,' said Xander.

'What does the gynaecologist say?'

'He can't find anything wrong with her. Joan wants her to have a second opinion—nice if she had an opinion at all. So the onus falls firmly on me. Pamela takes her temperature every morning, and when it goes up I'm supposed to pounce on her, but I always oversleep, or have debilitating hangovers, or don't get home like last night. But I've a feeling nothing's going to happen while I lie on one side of the bed reading Dick Francis, and she lies on the other poring over gardening books.'

He was rattling now. His hand shook as he lit a cigarette. I could sense his utter despair.

'Is it absolute hell?' I asked.

He shrugged. 'I suppose prep school was worse, but at least one had longer holidays then.'

'Don't worry,' I said. 'She'll get pregnant soon.'

Xander was busy ordering coffee and brandies and I was easing a piece of bacon out of my teeth, when I looked up and saw a boy of about twenty-three standing in the doorway. He had dark Shelley-length hair, huge languorous dark eyes, and a Mediterranean suntan. He wore navy blue pinstripe trousers and was carrying his jacket slung across his shoulders. His pale blue shirt was open at the neck to reveal a jungle of gold medallions nestling in a black hairy chest. He looked like a movie star. For a second I felt a flicker of unfaithfulness to Jeremy.

38

'Look at that,' I breathed to Xander.

'I'm already looking,' said Xander, and suddenly there was a touch of colour in his pale cheeks, as the dark boy looked round, caught Xander's eye, waved, and wandered lazily towards us.

'See a pinstripe suit, and pick him up, and all the day you'll have good luck,' murmured Xander.

'Hi,' said the dark boy. 'I was worried I'd missed you. The traffic is terrible.'

He had a strong foreign accent, and was shooting me an openly hostile look, which became distinctly more friendly when Xander said,

'This is my sister, Octavia. Darling, this is Guido. He comes from Florence, I must say I learnt more on my first trip to Florence than during my whole time at Radley.'

Guido sat down and said he would have expected Xander to have such a beautiful sister. Xander had completely shed his black gloom now. He seemed greatly exhilarated.

'Guido works at the Wellington Gallery,' he said. 'He's in disgrace at the moment because he put his foot through a Sisley yesterday, stepping back to avoid the attentions of the gallery owner. Another large brandy and some more coffee,' he added to the waiter.

Guido was staring openly at Xander. His glance had flickered over me and passed on in that dismissive way a man would by-pass the woman's page in a newspaper, knowing it had nothing to offer him.

'How is your dear wife?' he said.

'Dear,' said Xander. 'She's busy putting in a swimming pool. You must come down for a weekend.'

Suddenly I felt *de trop*, and got to my feet.

'I must go,' I said.

'Must you?' said Xander, but without conviction.

Then he suddenly remembered. 'I was going to get you some money, wasn't I? Come on, we'll go and chat up Freddy, I'll be right back,' he said to Guido.

We found Freddy in the bar.

'Now,' said Xander, making sure he looked Freddy straight in the eye. 'Can you cash me a small cheque?'

'Of course. How much?'

'£200.'

Freddy didn't bat an eyelid. He pulled a thick pile of notes in a money clip out of his pockets, and laid twenty tenners on the bar.

'I'll have to date the cheque sometime after the first of the month; is that O.K.?'

'Sure,' said Freddy, soothingly. 'I can always sue you.'

Xander gave me the money and escorted me to the door. I thanked him profusely.

'Don't give it a thought,' he said. 'Now have a ball with Jeremy Fisher. But keep your options open and your legs shut, and don't rule out Gareth Llewellyn altogether; he could keep us both in a style to which we're totally unaccustomed. Don't you think,' he jerked his head in the direction of the dining room, 'that that is quite the most ravishing thing you've seen in years?'

'Yes, he is,' I said with a sinking heart, 'but for God's sake be careful, Xander.'

'And the same to you, darling. Give me a ring when you get back.'

And he was gone, trying to appear not to be in too much of a hurry to get upstairs.

I felt curiously flat and decided to wander along to Hatchards and buy some highbrow books to impress Jeremy on the boat.

5

By Friday evening I was golden brown all over and ready for action. I decided Xander was right, my best tack was to charm Gareth and get him on my side, and at five-thirty I was waiting for him with my three suitcases packed. I was wearing a wickedly expensive pink and white striped blazer with nothing underneath, white trousers, and cherry red boots. The blazer and boots were really both too hot to wear but I was only going to be driving in a car. I felt entirely satisfied with my appearance.

The minutes ticked by. Six came and went, half-past six, a quarter to seven. I vacillated between seething temper that Gareth was late on purpose, and worry that he might have lost my address.

At half-past seven the telephone went. 'This is Annabel Smith,' said a husky voice. 'I'm ringing for Mr. Llewellyn.'

'Where the hell is he?' I snapped.

'I'm afraid his meeting is going on longer than expected. Could you possibly jump in a taxi and come over here? The address is Llewellyn House, Great Seaton Street. I'll meet you on the ground floor and reimburse you for the taxi.'

Oh, the hateful, horrible, utterly bloody man! Why the hell had I piled up my car? No taxis were free when I telephoned, all the mini cabs were booked for the next hour. My make-up was beginning to run in the heat. It was no joke having to hump three huge suitcases into the street and wait half-an-hour for a taxi. My blazer was too hot, my new boots killing me. By the time I reached Llewellyn House I was gibbering with rage.

Mrs. Smith, in green, looking as cool as an iced gin and lime, was there to meet me.

'Come upstairs; you must be exhausted. Someone will put your luggage in Mr. Llewellyn's car. What a perfect weekend for going on the river,' she said as we climbed in the lift to the fifteenth floor. I had a feeling she was amused.

I was ushered into an office as modern as the hour. There were some good modern paintings on the wall, leather armchairs with chrome legs, one wall covered in books and facing it a vast window, a cinemascopic frame for St. Paul's and the city. How could anyone work with a view like that? Gareth evidently could. He was lounging behind a huge black leathertopped desk, on the telephone as usual, talking execrable French.

He grinned and jabbed a paper in the direction of one of the armchairs. I ignored him and went over to the window. Buses like dinky toys were crawling up Fleet Street.

Mrs. Smith came in with a tray. 'Would you like a drink?'

I didn't want to take anything of Gareth's but I needed that drink too badly.

'Gin and tonic, please.'

She mixed me one with ice and lemon, and then poured a large whisky for Gareth.

He put down the receiver and smiled at me.

'Hullo, lovely. I'm sorry I've messed you about.' There wasn't a trace of contrition in his voice. 'You look stunning. It's as good as a day in the country just to see you.'

'I've been waiting nearly three hours,' I spat at him. 'Shall we go?'

He wandered towards the door taking his whisky with him. 'I'm going to have a shower first; make yourself at home.'

Mrs. Smith brought me some magazines. I thumbed through them furiously, not taking in a word.

It was nine o'clock by the time he came back, looking more like a lorry driver than ever, in jeans and a red shirt. He kissed Mrs. Smith very tenderly before we left.

'I see you believe in mixing business with pleasure,' I snapped as we went down in the lift.

'But of course. You wouldn't expect me to sit looking at some top-heavy frump in basic black all day, would you? That's a nice blazer you're wearing. Did you think we were going to Henley?'

'Oh this, it's as old as the hills.' I was damned if I was going to admit I'd bought it that morning.

He reached out his hand towards the back of my neck and pulled something off my collar.

'Don't touch me,' I hissed.

He handed me a price tag with a hundred pounds on it.

'If this is a cleaning ticket, darling, I'm afraid you've been robbed.'

I was furious to find myself blushing.

Outside the vulgarest car I've ever seen stood waiting for us, a vast open Cadillac sprayed a brilliant shade of peacock blue. I was surprised he hadn't hung nodding doggies from the driving mirror.

I had to admit he was a good driver, threading that huge car through the traffic in no time. We were soon out on the M4 speeding towards Oxford.

The sun had set. In the west were great masses of crushed-up rose-coloured clouds. Broad beams of light shone down, reminding me of an old biblical picture. If God were up there this evening dispensing justice, I hoped He'd give Gareth his come-uppance. And He might grant me Jeremy at the same time.

The needle on the speedometer registered a hundred m.p.h.

'Let me know if you're frightened and I'll go a bit faster,' said Gareth.

I stared stonily ahead.

'Oh pack it in, lovely; stop sulking. We've got to spend the weekend together, we might as well call a truce.'

'Why didn't you let me go earlier with the others?'

'Because I couldn't resist it—I wanted to annoy you. Never mind, I'll buy you a nice dinner.'

'I don't want any dinner.'

'All right, then, you can watch me eat.'

He pulled in at an hotel beyond Henley. It was obviously very expensive. Waiters were flambee-ing ducks all over the place and the menus had no prices on them. I suddenly realized I hadn't eaten all day and found my mouth was watering.

Gareth grinned at me. 'Come on, eat; you might as well.'

'Oh, all right,' I said.

Reluctantly I had to admit the food was excellent.

'I always eat well,' he said.

'So I notice,' I said, looking at his waist line.

He roared with laughter. 'I suppose you like little mini boys with hip measurements in single figures, but as Freddie Trueman once said, it takes a big hammer to drive a big nail.'

'Don't be disgusting,' I snapped.

His table manners were atrocious. Somehow he managed to eat very fast and talk at the same time. Now he was draining butter out of his snail shells with a sound like water running out of the bath. God, it was hot in the restaurant. I was pouring with sweat but I could hardly take my blazer off.

'I had lunch with Jeremy, yesterday,' he said, wiping butter off his chin.

'Oh, I'm surprised you found the time.'

'I always find time for things that matter. I think I've found them a house.'

'That's clever of you,' I said coolly. 'Whereabouts?'

'Kensington, round the corner from me.'

'How can they afford it? Jeremy hasn't got that kind of money.'

'But Gussie has. She's going to buy the house.'

'Jeremy'd loathe that.'

'Not now, he doesn't. I've managed to persuade him how sensible it is. They can let out the bottom floor which will pay off the mortgage, and it means they can get married next month instead of waiting until November.'

His face had that dreamy far-away look of a volcano that has just devastated entire villages. I wanted to kick his teeth in but I was determined not to betray any emotion.

'They must be thrilled,' I said.

'Yes they are. I expect Gussie'll ask you to be a bridesmaid.'

I couldn't speak for rage. I was glad when the pretty

44

waitress came over. 'Everything all right sir?' She smiled at him admiringly.

'Marvellous.' He looked her over in a way that made me even angrier.

'How much further have we got to go?' I asked as we got back into the car.

'Twenty, thirty miles, not more.'

The stars were of Mediterranean splendour now, the newly cut hay smelt sweet, feathery moths were held prisoner in the beams of the powerful headlights. The air, cool at fast speeds, grew hot again whenever Gareth slowed down to take a corner. We were driving past the Reedminster flyover now.

'Look,' said Gareth, pointing upwards. On a huge floodlit placard was written the word 'Llewellyns'.

'You?' I said, in surprise.

'Me. I'll be bigger than Taylor Woodrow one day.'

'Quite the boy wonder. Why do you go on working so hard? You've made your packet. Why's it so important to make more money?'

'Oh lovely, you must be weak in the head. For heaven's sake, if you play a game, even if it's only scrabble, you want to win don't you?'

'And it matters so much to you, the winning?'

'Of course it does, why not have a Lamborghini and a Rolls Royce and a nice house in London, and a villa in France? And if you can throw in a few good paintings, a string of race horses, the odd yacht in the Med, well bully for you.'

'It's status symbols that really matter to you don't they?'

'And to you too,' said Gareth. 'More than anyone, you need a sybaritic existence with different guys to take you to trendy restaurants, buy you fur coats, fly you to all the smart places. It wouldn't amuse you at all to be shackled to a poor man.'

I opened my mouth to protest, but he went on.

'Jeremy's the same. He's lucky to be marrying Gus, who's got some bread.'

'Jeremy'll make money out of writing,' I said quickly.

'Nuts! He can't write "bum" on a wall. I bet you don't understand a word of those poems of his you claim to be so fond of, and do you know why? It's because there isn't anything in them *to* understand.'

'I can only assume you must be jealous of his talent,' I said furiously.

'Oh, don't be pompous, sweetheart. There's far more poetry in those blue eyes of his than there is in any of his verse.'

'I thought you were supposed to be a friend of his?'

'So I am, but I believe in doing practical things for him like getting him somewhere to live, rather than swooning over his tin-pot poetry.'

I didn't trust myself to speak. Gareth said, 'We'll be there in ten minutes.'

I started to do my face.

He flicked on a spotlight to help me, then said, 'Go easy on the warpaint.'

'Why?' I asked, painting a more seductive curve on my bottom lip.

'Because Jeremy belongs to Gussie.'

'And?'

'You've come down with the sole purpose of getting him away from her.'

'I don't know what you mean.'

'Oh yes you do. That performance you two were putting on the other night, not speaking to each other when anyone else was around, rushing together as soon as you were alone. I heard you both: "Oh darling, we shall have to rely on self-control." '

It was a brilliant imitation of my voice.

'Gussie is an old friend,' I said evenly.

'That's the trouble, you're jealous of her.'

'Jealous. Me jealous of Gussie? You must be joking!'

'Because, despite your looks, people love her more than they do you.'

'That's not true,' I said through gritted teeth. 'Gussie is a friend and I couldn't be less interested in Jeremy.'

'Good,' said Gareth amiably. 'Keep it that way then. Here we are.'

46

He turned off the road down a long woody tunnel. Clenching my hands, I choked back the torrent of rage and fury that was ready to pour out of me. Jeremy's mad for you, I said to myself, keep calm. Gareth's just trying to bug you. Gareth stretched.

'What a marvellous prospect, three whole days of sleep, sex and sun.'

'It isn't very likely,' I hissed, 'that you'll get any sex from me.'

'Not likely at all, unless I ask you for it,' he said.

Just as I was groping for a really crushing reply, we emerged out of the tunnel and found ourselves almost at the water's edge. The sky unfurled like a banner cascading with stars. Black hulks of barges darkened the water. Behind, the murky towers and pinnacles of Oxford rose indistinctly.

Jeremy emerged from the nearest boat to meet us. I'd never felt more pleased to see anyone. I wanted to throw myself sobbing into his arms.

'Hullo,' he said. 'You made it okay? Let me help with the cases.'

'I'm desperately sorry we're so late,' I said.

'Doesn't matter. Gareth rang this afternoon and said you wouldn't be here much before midnight.'

In the headlamps of the car I could see the barge was painted scarlet and decorated in brilliant blues, yellows and greens, like a gypsy caravan. The brasswork glinted, the red curtains glowed behind the saloon windows. In gold letters edged with blue was written her name, *The Lady Griselda*.

'Isn't she lovely?' I said.

Jeremy helped me across the gangplank, but he didn't squeeze my hand, nor answer when I whispered that it was heavenly to see him again.

Gussie was in the kitchen. She was wearing old jeans and an oil-stained shirt. I suddenly realized how stupid I must look bringing three suitcases.

'Tavy,' she hugged me. 'How lovely. Have you been having fun?'

'Yes, marvellous,' I lied, disengaging myself from her. I didn't want oil stains all over my new blazer.

'You must be exhausted. Come and see your cabin, and then I'll give you a huge drink.'

We went through a cabin with two bunks in it.

'This is Jeremy and me,' she said, and then opening another door, 'This is you and Gareth.'

Oh, my God, I thought, I'm going to have to spend the whole weekend fighting him off. Our suitcases were already deposited on one of the bunks. On a ledge stood a glass jam jar which Gussie had filled with meadow sweet, buttercups and already wilting roses.

'The heads and the washbasin are next door. I'm afraid they're a bit primitive, and the saloon's beyond that,' she said. 'Come through when you're ready.'

I washed and put on more scent and make-up to give me confidence. In the saloon I found them all gathered round a portable television set.

'Look at Gareth's toy,' said Gussie.

'Trust him to bring the twentieth century with him,' I said and looked at Jeremy, but he looked quickly away.

'Have a drink?' said Gussie.

'I'll get her one,' said Gareth, getting a glass out of a cupboard in the corner and filling it with wine.

'Isn't this gorgeous?' I said, looking round at the oil lamps, the panelling and the gleaming brass.

'Very sexy too,' added Gareth approvingly. 'Octavia and I are waking at the crack of dawn to do PT.'

'PT?' said Gussie in surprise. 'That doesn't sound Octavia's line of country.'

'Some people call it sexual intercourse,' said Gareth.

He raised his glass to me, his wicked lecherous eyes moving over me in amusement.

Gussie went off into peals of laughter.

'You mustn't tease, Gareth. Poor Tavy won't know if she's coming or going.'

'Coming, hopefully,' said Gareth.

48

'I hear you've found a house,' I said to Jeremy. 'I'm so pleased.'

For a moment he looked up and our eyes met, then he looked quickly away. A muscle was going in his cheek; he was obviously in a state.

'Yes, it's great, isn't it?'

'Great!' said Gussie, 'it's marvellous! Most couples can't afford a house for years. Gareth fixed us a mortgage and found us the ideal place in a few days. You must come and help me choose curtains and carpets, Tavy. I'm so hopeless.'

They started talking about the house and wedding plans until I couldn't stand it any more. 'Does anyone mind if I go to bed?' I said.

'Of course not,' said Gussie. 'I'll come and see everything's all right.'

'You'll see me anon,' said Gareth.

'No doubt,' I said, turning to Jeremy, 'Goodnight, it's such a treat to be down here.'

Just for a moment I was comforted by a flicker of misery in his eyes, then the shutters came down.

'Goodnight, sleep well,' he said.

In my cabin, Gussie was plumping pillows.

'It was a good thing Gareth rang Jeremy and said you were going to be late, or we'd have been in an awful shambles. Jeremy and I spent all afternoon in bed,' Gussie confided with a little giggle, then went on, 'I hope you don't mind sharing a cabin with Gareth. I'm sure he won't pounce on you unless you want it.'

'What on earth do you mean?' I snapped.

'Oh well,' she stammered. 'I mean, I thought you might want it, perhaps, if you found him attractive.'

'I don't,' I said.

'Oh dear,' her face fell. Realizing it was a bad move, I added, 'I like him very much, but not in that way.'

Once I was alone, I couldn't stop shaking. What had that snake Gareth been saying to Jeremy to change him so much? Had he just done it out of sheer bloodymindedness or did he

49

want me for himself? When I was in my nightie (which was apricot silk, clinging and, ironically, bought to inflame Jeremy) I found to my horror that I had left my sleeping pills behind. In the state I was in I'd never sleep without them.

I put all my suitcases on the floor, and crept into the top bunk and lay there, tense and trembling, waiting to fend off the inevitable assault when Gareth came to bed. All I could hear were shouts of laughter from the other room.

An hour went past; they were coming to bed; there were shouts of 'goodnight', then silence, broken only by the sound of water lapping against the boat.

The door opened, and Gareth slid quietly into the cabin. Hoping he would not hear the terrified thudding of my heart, I tried to breathe slowly and evenly.

'Only five out of ten,' came the soft Welsh voice. 'People who are really asleep breathe much faster than that.'

Then, to my amazement, I heard him getting into the bottom bunk. He must be trying to lull me into a feeling of false security. I lay frozen for ten minutes, but suddenly my terror turned to fury. Unmistakably from the bottom bunk came the sound of gentle snoring.

I lay there spitting with rage until eventually I decided it was no use working myself up into a state. Gareth might have temporarily chucked a monkey wrench into the romantic works, but if he intended to fight dirty, he would find that no one could fight dirtier than me when I put my mind to it. Whatever he had told Jeremy—that I was a spoilt bitch, a parasite, an opportunist—would make no difference in the end. Jeremy was mad for me, try as he might to fight it.

Time was on my side. In this heat, cooped up together for three days, Jeremy's self-control was bound to desert him. All I had to do was look stunning and wait. *Festina lente.* But how could I be expected to look stunning if I couldn't sleep? I wanted to go up on the moonlit deck and cool off. But although Gareth was now snoring like a warthog, I had a feeling that as soon as I tried to climb out of my bunk, his hand would shoot out and grab me by the ankle. Why, oh why, had I forgotten to bring my sleeping pills? The hours crawled by, and only when a misty dawn began to filter through the porthole, did I fall asleep.

6

When I woke the boat was moving. Through the porthole I could see shiny olive-green water, a tangle of rushes and brilliant blue sky. I could hear voices and the crash of footsteps above me. I pulled the sheets over my head and tried to go back to sleep again, then gave up and looked at my watch. It was nearly twelve o'clock.

When I pushed open the door of the loo I was confronted by a huge brown back and tousled black hair. Gareth, wearing only a towel around his hips, was cleaning his teeth.

'You're up with the lark,' he said grinning. 'You *must* have slept well.'

'Don't you ever wear any pyjamas?' I snapped.

'Never, never. I always sleep in the raw. I like to get really close to people. Shall I run you a bath, or would you prefer a shower? I'll see if Gussie's got any Badedas.'

Knowing there was only a cracked wash basin, I ignored this and flattened myself against the wall to let him pass. He paused in front of me and once again I was overwhelmed by the claustrophobia I always felt when he was close to me. As I bolted past him and locked the door behind me, I could hear him laughing.

He'd gone, thank goodness, when I got back to the cabin. I couldn't decide what to wear, all my clothes looked so new. In

51

the end I settled for a dark green towelling jump suit with a red and green striped leather belt.

Gussie was in the kitchen, cooking and pinkfaced. 'Hello,' she said. 'How are you? Did you sleep all right?'

She was obviously dying to know if I'd slept with Gareth or not, and was on the look out for signs of ravage in my face.

'I fell asleep the moment my head touched the pillow,' I said blithely. 'Can I do anything to help?'

'No, don't bother. Do you want some breakfast?'

'Only a cup of coffee.'

'You ought to eat something, you know,' she insisted.

'I can't even look a fried egg in the face in the morning.'

She began boringly explaining to me the merits of eating a proper breakfast, so I made a cup of coffee and a quick exit up on deck.

A beautiful burning day had soared out of the mist. On either side white cornfields slanted down to the water, ahead on the left bank a clump of copper beeches glittered purple in the sun. The water ahead was so smooth, it was as though we were gliding over an old mirror. Jeremy, wearing only a pair of jeans, was at the wheel. He looked all tawny and golden haired, like a young lion, but his dark blue eyes were tired.

'Everything all right?' he said.

'Yes, thank you, everything's wonderful.' I gave him a smile of pure happiness. Let him sweat, I thought, let him have a few nasty moments wondering if I really have been screwed by Gareth.

'You look very pleased with yourself,' said a soft Welsh voice. Gareth sat hunched up on the roof, his arms round his knees, smoking and reading the *Financial Times*.

'How the hell did you get hold of that?' I asked.

'From the last lock-keeper, a man of property like myself.'

'Anything up?' asked Jeremy.

'My shares are, by 10p,' said Gareth.

'Don't you ever let up?' I said.

'Only in the mating season.'

'Jeremee,' called Gussie from the kitchen.

'Yes love?'

'You haven't kissed me for at least a quarter-of-an-hour.'

Jeremy looked at us and blushed.

'Get on with it, you fleshmonger,' said Gareth, getting to his feet. 'I'll take the wheel.'

'We'll be coming up to Ramsdyke Lock in half-an-hour,' said Jeremy. 'I'll come and take over then.'

He went dutifully down into the kitchen.

'In a few years' time,' I said savagely, 'they'll be calling each other "Mummy" and "Daddy".'

I enjoyed going through the lock. The lock-keeper's little house was surrounded by a garden of flowers as gaudy as the front of a seed packet. A goat looked over the fence, a golden retriever sat lolling its tongue out in the heat. When Jeremy sounded the horn a fat woman in an apron came out and opened the first lot of gates for us. Then the boat edged its way into the dark green cavern with dank slimy walls and purple toadflax growing in the crevices, and the gates clanged behind us. Suddenly water poured in from the other end, gradually raising our boat to the new level of the river.

'Very phallic, isn't it?' said Gareth, who was waiting on the shore to open the gates at the other end.

I looked up at him with loathing. 'Do you keep your mind permanently below your navel?'

We tied up for lunch under a veil of green willows, and I changed into my favourite bikini, which is that stinging yellow which goes so well with brown skin and blonde hair, and very cleverly cut to give me a cleavage like the Grand Canyon.

'Hickory dickory dock, the mouse ran up the drink bill,' said Gareth, pouring himself a quadruple whisky. 'This weekend is fast degenerating into an orgy.'

He looked up and whistled as I walked into the saloon.

'Despite your obvious limitations, Octavia, I must admit that you're very well constructed. Really, it's a sin for you to wear any clothes at all. Don't you agree Jeremy?'

Jeremy was devouring me, as a starved dog might look at a large steak. His hand shook as he lit a cigarette, that muscle was going in his cheek again.

'Oh these engaged men never look at other women,' I said lightly. 'Pour me a drink, Gareth darling.'

We all got tight at lunch. It was far too hot to eat but as Gussie had spent all morning making a fish mayonnaise, we had to make half-hearted efforts. She'd even cut the tomatoes into little flowers. As usual she ended up by guzzling most of it herself.

Afterwards, as Jeremy and Gareth cast off, I curled up in a sunbaked corner on deck. A few minutes later Gussie joined me—not a pretty sight in a black bathing dress, her huge white bosom and shoulders spilling over the top. She immediately started boring me making lists for her wedding.

'There's so much to do with only a month to go,' she kept saying. How many double sheets did I think she'd need, and was it absolutely essential to have an egg beater? But her fond dreamy gaze rested more often on Jeremy than on her lists.

'Isn't he beautiful?' she said, then giggled. 'Gareth's given me this fantastic sex instruction book. I can now see why so many people end up with slipped discs. The things they expect you to do, and it's a bit tricky when you have to hold the book in one hand in order to learn how to do it,' and she went off into shrieks of laughter.

'How are you getting on with Gareth?' she went on.

I admired my reflection in her sun glasses. 'Well I'm not getting off with him, if that's what you mean.'

'Ah—but the weekend is still in its infancy,' said that hateful Welsh voice and Gareth lay down on the deck between us, cushioning his dark head on his elbow, the wicked slit eyes staring up at the burning sky.

'I've just been telling Tavy about your fantastic sex book,' said Gussie.

'I wouldn't have thought she'd need it,' said Gareth. 'She must have taken her "L" plates off years ago.'

A large white barge was cruising towards us on the other side of the river. A middle-aged man in a yachting cap was at the wheel, addressing two fat women with corrugated hair up at

54

the front of the boat, through a speaking trumpet. Another man with a white moustache and a red face was gazing at us through binoculars. They all looked thoroughly disapproving. Gareth sat up and waited until they drew level with us.

'Have a good look, sir!' he shouted to the man with the binoculars. 'I've got two lovely young girls here, whose knickers are bursting into flames at the sight of you. Only fifty quid each, satisfaction guaranteed. We even accept Barclay Cards.'

The man with the binoculars turned purple with rage and nearly fell off the roof.

'It's young men like you who ought to be turned off England's waterways!' bellowed the man with the speaking trumpet.

'We even take luncheon vouchers!' Gareth yelled after them.

'I'll ask you along instead of a conjurer next time I give a children's party,' I said.

Gussie, who was doubled up with laughter, got to her feet.

'I'm going to see how Jeremy's getting on,' she said.

I buried my face in my biography of Matthew Arnold.

'Still on the culture kick?' said Gareth in amusement. 'There's only one poem, lovely, you should read, learn and inwardly digest.'

'What's that?'

' "Who ever loves, if he do not
        propose
    The right true end of love, he's one
        that goes
    To sea for nothing but to make
        him sick." '

'Who wrote that?'

'Your alleged favourite, John Donne.'

'He must have been having an off day,' I said crossly.

Another boat passed us with a pretty brunette sunning herself on deck. Gareth wolf-whistled at her; she turned round and smiled at him, showing big teeth. Gareth smiled back.

'Don't you ever knock it off,' I snapped. 'Haven't you ever

heard of the law of diminishing returns?'

A dark green world slid past my half-shut eyes. The darkness of the trees over-arched the olive shadows and tawny lights of the water. On the bank was a large notice: 'Danger. Keep Away from the Weir.'

'It's not the weir that some people should keep away from,' said Gareth.

Beyond the weir, the surface of the river was smothered in foam, a floating rainbow coloured like gossamer.

'Oh how pretty it is!' I cried.

'Detergent,' said Gareth.

I shot him a venomous glance and started fiddling with my wireless. I'd given up listening to pop music since I'd met Jeremy, but suddenly I hit upon some grand opera, a soprano and a tenor yelling their guts out. I was just about to switch over when Gareth looked up. 'For Christ sake turn that cater-wauling off. You'll wake up all the water rats.'

So I kept it on really loud to annoy him, absolutely murder-ing the peace of the afternoon. After an agonizing three-quarters of an hour, the opera came to an end.

'What was that?' bellowed Gussie from the wheel.

'Don Carlos,' I said.

'Oh how lovely! That's your favourite, isn't it, Gareth? How many times have you seen it?'

The rat! The snake! Smiling damned villain! I couldn't trust myself to speak. I turned over and pretended to go to sleep.

I was lying half drugged with sun when I heard Jeremy's voice. 'Octavia, are you asleep?'

I opened my eyes; the sky was shimmering with heat. I smiled lazily up at him. From the ribald laughter I could hear, Gareth and Gussie were obviously up at the other end of the boat.

Jeremy sat down beside me.

'You must watch the sun. With fair skin like yours, you could easily burn.'

'Oil me then,' I said softly, turning over on my front and handing him a bottle of Ambre Solaire.

He put a dollop on his hands and began to rub it into my back.

I squirmed voluptuously. 'Oh, how blissful. I wish I had a tame slave to do it all the time. Put lots on the tops of my thighs,' I went on mercilessly. I heard him catch his breath.

When I had made him spin it out as long as possible, I added, 'And could you possibly undo my bikini strap. I don't want a white line across my back.'

His hands shook so much he had the greatest difficulty with the clasp.

'Thank you,' I said when he had finished, turning my head and looking at him. He was breathing very fast, and his eyes were almost opaque with lust.

The afternoon was perfect now. The water was plumed with alders and willows, and in the distance two or three pink farm houses dozed among the apple trees. The white spire of a village church appeared behind a hill and a plane sailed silver across the sky.

'How remote everything seems,' I said. 'I can't believe that this time next week I shall be in Marbella.'

Jeremy sat up on his elbow, chewing a piece of grass.

'You will?'

'And Sardinia the week after, and then I think I shall probably take off for Bermuda for the summer.'

'Bermuda? Whatever for?'

I was taunting him now.

'Oh, because a guy with whom I'm just good friends is mad for me to join him out there. He was even generous enough to send me my air ticket.'

'Doesn't it worry you at all? Living off men all the time?'

'Who said I'm living off men? I give as good as I get. Anyway it's only normal if one's father rejects one early in life, to go round looking for other daddies, preferably sugar daddies and playing them up until they're forced to reject you too.'

'Don't you ever want to settle down with one man?'

'Not any more,' I paused, making my voice quiver slightly. 'Not since Tod was killed earlier this year.'

'Gussie told me about that. I'm terribly sorry.'

A yellow butterfly shimmered over us. 'That's me,' I said, pointing to it. 'Always on the loose.'

'So you're really committed to the fleshpots,' said Jeremy bitterly. 'Drifting from one rich playboy to another. Dropping your knickers so you don't have to drop your standard of living.'

'That sounds exactly like Gareth,' I said through my teeth. 'It's neither funny nor true.'

'Maybe not. Now you can have as many minks and gold bracelets as you like, but what happens when your looks go and you can't get men any more? Do you know how women like you end up, unless they're very careful? They start making concessions in order to escape from their loneliness, then more and more concessions until they turn into a raddled old harridan that everyone laughs at.'

'Why do you tell me these things?' I hissed at him.

'It's only natural,' he said in a low voice, 'that I should try and run down all the things I could never afford to give you.'

'Gareth could give them to me,' I said.

'What happened between you two last night?' he said sharply.

'Oh, you know Gareth's reputation, and you think mine is totally beyond redemption, I'm surprised you ask.'

'What happened?' he said, seizing my wrist.

'Stop it, you're hurting me!'

'Did you or did you not sleep with Gareth?'

'No I didn't, but it's no thanks to you,' I stormed. 'Ignoring me when we arrived last night, avoiding my eyes whenever I looked at you. If anything was calculated to throw me into Gareth's arms that was.'

Jeremy put his face in his hands.

'I know, I know. Christ I'm in such a muddle. A month today I'm getting married, and I feel as though I'm going into hospital for a major operation.'

'Well, that's your problem, isn't it?' I said, fastening my

58

bikini strap and getting to my feet. 'I'm going to get a drink of water.'

I found Gussie in the kitchen eating biscuits and talking up at Gareth who was steering.

'Gussie and I were just saying how much we were looking forward to sampling some of your famous cooking,' said Gareth maliciously.

'There's a chicken in the fridge,' said Gussie. 'I wish you'd do that marvellous thing you did when Jeremy and I came to dinner.'

'It's a very complicated recipe,' I said quickly, 'and needs lots of special things I'm sure we haven't got.'

'We can get them,' said Gussie. 'Gareth and I have got a yen for Pimms tonight, so we thought we'd stop off at the village shop at the next lock. We'll buy everything you need at the same time.'

I hope my dismay didn't show on my face. While Gareth and Gussie were shopping, I had a good wash to get off all the sun-tan oil and sweat. I was just wandering into the kitchen to get another glass of water when I felt something furry run across my feet. I gave a scream. Jeremy came racing down the passage.

'What's the matter?'

'Look,' I screamed. A huge spider ran across the floor and disappeared under the sink.

'It's only a spider,' he said. 'It won't hurt you.'

'They terrify me,' I sobbed. He took a step towards me and then the next moment I was in his arms. As his lips touched mine, we both began to tremble. The warmth, the dizziness, the taste of that kiss lasted a long, long time. Then he buried his face in my hair.

'Oh my God, Octavia, you're driving me mad. What am I going to do?'

'Nothing for the moment, except go on kissing me,' I whispered, taking his face in my hands.

7

The crimson sun was sinking, the pink water darkening as we tied up for the night alongside a bank of meadowsweet. The air throbbed with the formless chattering of birds, and all along the bank water rats and owls began to come out on night duty. I managed to postpone cooking by saying the chicken would take too long to make.

I put on a pale grey semi-transparent mini-dress. I didn't need the cracked looking glass to tell me how marvellous I looked. Gussie was looking hideous in white. She was scarlet from the sun.

'She looks like a great red lobster,' I thought with a giggle. 'All she needs is a dollop of mayonnaise.'

Gareth handed me a Pimms. It was afloat with apple, cucumber and oranges.

'Is this dinner as well?' I asked coolly.

'It's utterly divine,' said Gussie. 'Try it.'

I took a sip and smirked at Gareth. 'It tastes exactly like cough mixture,' I said.

Jeremy, sitting at the table shelling broad beans, looked fantastic. His skin was tanned to the colour of dry sherry; he was wearing a white shirt. I surreptitiously lowered the zip of my dress a few inches, then caught Gareth looking at me and pretended I was fanning myself because of the heat.

'Jeremy darling,' cooed Gussie fondly, 'you're putting all the pods in the pan and the beans in the muckbucket. You *are* abstracted today.'

'His mind's on other things,' said Gareth.

'Like this bloody review I've got to write for the *Statesman*,' said Jeremy. 'I've got to file copy on Tuesday. I simply can't get beyond the first chapter.'

'Well say so, then,' said Gareth

'I can't,' said Jeremy. 'It was written by the editor's wife.'

'That's a gorgeous dress,' said Gussie, looking at me enviously. 'I'd love something really sexy like that.'

'You've got Jeremy,' I said, smiling at him.

'Yes, and don't let any of us forget it,' said Gareth.

'Broad beans are disappointing,' grumbled Gussie, raking her thumb nail down the furry inside of the last pod. 'They always look as though they're going to produce far more than they do.'

'Like someone else I could mention,' muttered Gareth as he filled up my glass.

A smell of mint drifted in from the kitchen.

'I'm starving,' said Gussie.

For dinner Gareth fried some huge prawns in garlic and parsley and we ate them with broad beans and new potatoes.

'Our new house has a little garden,' said Gussie with her mouth full. 'Just think Jeremy darling, we'll be able to grow our own vegetables. You're a fairy godmother, Gareth, finding us this house.'

'I'm neither a fairy nor a godmother,' said Gareth, forking a large new potato out of the dish and putting it straight into his mouth.

'These prawns are fantastic,' said Jeremy. 'Have some more, Octavia.'

'No thanks,' I said. 'I'm surprised to see Gareth cooking at all. With your pithead upbringing I'd have thought you'd have been dead against men in the kitchen.'

There was a slightly embarrassed pause.

'My father spent his time in the kitchen when he was home,' said Gareth. 'It was the only room we had downstairs.'

'How amazing,' I said, my lips curling. 'Did you all sleep in the same bed?'

'I liked your father,' said Jeremy hastily.

'So did my mother,' said Gareth. 'If you're a miner you're a real man—and women like that.'

Gussie sensed that I was about to make some crushing remark.

'Whatever happened to your glamorous brother?' she said. 'I remember him coming down to take you out at school and watching a lacrosse match, and no one scoring any goals at all. They were far too busy gawping at him.'

'He went into the family business,' I said. 'But he hates it. He's export sales manager now and has to spend his time swapping filthy stories with reps.'

'Who did he get married to?' said Gussie.

'Ricky Seaford's daughter, Pamela.'

'That was a good dynastic match,' said Gareth. 'Aren't Seaford-Brennen's in a bit of trouble at the moment?'

'Of course not,' I said, scathingly. 'They've had a terrific year.' I always say that.

'Oh well, you should know,' said Gareth. 'I just heard rumours of strike trouble.'

'All firms have to cope with strikes from time to time.'

'I don't,' said Gareth, grinning. 'My men know they've got the best boss in the world, so why should they strike?'

'Modesty certainly isn't your strong point,' I snapped.

'Of course it isn't. I'm much better at being immodest.'

God, he irritated me. I wanted to throw my drink in his face. Gussie went off to bring in some strawberries and cream, so I stretched out my foot towards Jeremy and started rubbing it against his leg. The pressure was immediately returned. And when Gareth started quizzing him about publishing, he obviously had great difficulty in concentrating.

'These are the first strawberries of the year, so you must all make a wish,' said Gussie, doling out great platefuls.

I wriggled down a bit further under the table, and ran my leg up and down Jeremy's thigh. The next moment I could feel his hand stroking my foot, gently caressing the instep. It felt fantastically sexy. I wiggled my toes against his hand voluptuously.

'Did you know that buggery was legal after 90 days on board?' said Gareth. 'So we've only got 89 days to go, boyo.'

'Oh darling,' sighed Jeremy, 'I never knew you felt that way.'

That warm hand was still stroking my ankle. Then suddenly I looked across the table, and froze with horror as I realized that Jeremy was squashing up his strawberries with both hands. Before I could whip my foot away, the hand had closed round my ankle like a vice.

'What big feet you've got Grandma,' said Gareth, his eyes glinting with laughter. I tugged frantically for several seconds before he let me go.

After dinner he turned on the television. It was an old film, *Carmen Jones*.

'*You go for me, and I'm taboo,*' sang Dorothy Dandridge, shaking her hips, '*But if you're hard to get I go for you . . . and if I do, I'll tell you baby, that's the end of you.*'

'Oh, turn it off, I've seen it twice already,' said Gussie.

We took our drinks out on deck. The trees on the edge of the river were as dark as blackberries. A little owl swooped by noisily. A slight breeze wafted the strong soapy scent of the meadowsweet towards us. In the distance we could hear the sensual throb of pop music, and see the dark sky florid like a great bruise.

'It's a fair,' said Gussie in excitement. 'Oh, please let's go.'

The red and yellow helter-skelter rose like a fairy tower out of the pale green chestnut trees, the lights of the big wheel turned like a giant firework. I listened to the beat of the music, the roar of the generators and the thwack of balls on the canvas at the back of the coconut shies. I'm always turned on by fairs.

Gareth had just loosened every tooth in my head, driving like James Hunt round the dodgem car track. My only consolation was that Jeremy and Gussie, now clutching a Gary Glitter poster, a china Alsatian and a huge mauve teddy bear, had been watching our progress. Next to them had stood a group of youths who had wolf-whistled and whooped in admiration every time we crashed past them, as my hair whipped back and my skirt blew up to reveal an expanse of brown thigh. This was the kind of corporate approval that wouldn't do Jeremy any harm. Now Gareth was wasting a fortune at the shooting range, and Jeremy and I stood side by side watching Gussie riding on a merry-go-round horse with red nostrils. Grasping the brass rod with both hands, her handbag flying on her arm, her eyes shining, she smiled at us every time she came past. We smiled dutifully back.

The sensual beat of the music was eating into my soul. It was now or never. Out of the corner of my eye I saw the big wheel pause to take on more passengers. Gussie's merry-go-round would stop in a minute.

'Let's go on the big wheel,' I said to Jeremy.

'Won't you be scared?'

'Not with you.'

'We must be careful. Gussie'll start suspecting something.'

'I want her to,' I said.

With almost indecent haste, we slid into the bucket seats. At that moment Gussie clambered off her horse and looked round.

'Over here,' shouted Jeremy.

She looked up and grinned. 'Take care,' she shouted.

Up and up went the wheel. At the top we could see for miles. The moon had broken free from its moorings and was sailing up in the sky. Below us lay lit-up villages, dark woods, pale hayfields, and to the right, the distant gleam of the river.

'Oh isn't it beautiful?' I said, moving my leg against his.

'Beautiful,' he said, not looking at the view.

Then down we plunged with that dreadful stomach-stealing, heart-dropping fall. Screaming like a peacock, I clutched Jeremy's arm.

'Are you all right?' he said, as we swooped upwards again.

Then suddenly, fate came to our rescue. The wheel stopped to drop off some passengers, leaving us at the top, miles from everyone.

For a second we gazed at each other.

'What are you so frightened of?' I said softly. 'Gareth's disapproval or hurting Gussie?'

'Both. Gus doesn't deserve to be hurt, and I feel guilty

bringing Gareth down here, laying on a bird for him, then trying to lay on her myself.'

'You'd be insane with rage if I'd got off with Gareth.'

'I know I would.'

'Well then, is it fair to Gussie to marry her when you feel like this?'

'I think I'm more frightened of you than anything else,' he muttered. 'Like Carmen Jones on the box tonight, I'd be like that poor sod Don José. Once you got me away from Gussie you'd get bored with me. Then I'd find myself totally hooked on you, and not capable of holding you.'

'Oh darling,' I said, putting a little sob in my voice, 'don't you realize, I'm only playing the field because I'm unhappy? When I find the right guy, I'm quite capable of sticking to him. I was never unfaithful to Tod.'

'Not at all?'

'Not at all. You've got to learn to trust me.'

Jeremy looked up at the sky.

'I could reach up and pick you a bunch of stars,' he said. 'I wish we could stay up here forever and never go back to reality.'

The wheel started moving again.

'We've got to talk,' I whispered. 'Wait till Gussie's asleep and then creep up on deck.'

'It's too risky. Gareth's got a nose on elastic.'

'He's drunk so much this evening, he'll go out like a light.'

'Anyone want a drink?' said Gareth when we got back to the boat.

'I'm going to hit the hay,' said Jeremy. 'I've got a bloody awful headache from the sun.'

'I've got some pain killers in my suitcase,' said Gareth. 'I'll get them.'

He went out of the room. Gussie was rootling around in the kitchen. I moved towards Jeremy.

'Have you really got a headache?' I said.

He smiled slightly and shook his head: 'I ache in rather more

65

basic parts of my anatomy.'

'Painkillers won't cure that,' I said softly. 'The only remedy is to come up on deck later.'

'How long shall I leave it?'

'Well I certainly can't hold out for more than an hour,' I said, running my tongue over my lips.

At that moment Gareth returned with the pills.

'I really don't like taking things,' said Jeremy.

'You take three,' said Gareth firmly. 'That should do the trick.'

I'd have given anything to have a long scented bath. As it was, I stood barefoot on the rushmatting, soaping my body, and then dried myself with an old towel, the consistency of a brillo pad. I didn't even dare scent my body with bath oil, in case Gareth thought I was giving him the come on. But luckily when I went back to the cabin, he was already in bed, snoring away like Tommy Brock. I waited half an hour, then very slowly eased myself out of bed, groping for the wall and then the doorway. I had my alibi ready—I was just getting a drink of water—but I didn't need it. Gareth didn't stir. I tiptoed out of the cabin and up onto the deck.

The sullen heat of the torrid afternoon had given way to a blissful cool. Through the overhanging willows, the stars shone like blossom. I lay stretched out on the deck, listening to the soft gurgling of the river, the drowsy piping of birds, and the chatter and rustlings as the animals of night plied their trades. Half an hour passed in blissful expectation, then another half-hour when I knew he'd be here any minute.

What was that poem that always made us giggle at school?

He is coming, my dove, my dear:
He is coming, my life, my fate;
The red rose cries, 'He is near, he is near';
And the white rose weeps, 'He is late.'

Well it seemed the white rose had got the message all right. Another hour limped by, by which time the deck was harder

66

than a board, and fire was beginning to come out of my nostrils. It was obvious I was going to get no chance to play deck coitus. Anger gave way to misery and exhaustion, and I crept back to bed.

8

I was woken by the din of church bells. The cabin was already like an oven, the day far sunnier than my mood. I lay for a few seconds sourly wallowing in the bitterness of rejection. Master Jeremy, it had to be faced, had displayed thighs of clay. It was possible Gussie had had an attack of insomnia or intense amorousness last night, which had prevented him sneaking up on deck to find me, but it seemed unlikely. I had been convinced I could extract him from her as easily as a Kleenex from its box. But I had plainly miscalculated. He must prefer the security of her prop forward arms to my more subtle embraces. They were, after all, engaged, and he more accustomed to behaving like a gentleman than a full-blooded male. All the same, I wasn't going to give up without a fight; it would give old Torquemada Llewellyn too much satisfaction. I'd just have to find a chisel and prise Jeremy away like a barnacle.

The boat was also beginning to get on my nerves. My hair hadn't been washed for two days and was losing its slippery sheen. I was desperate to have a bath, and fed up with not being able to admire myself in a long mirror.

Gussie was in the kitchen—I'm surprised she didn't put up a camp bed there—simultaneously washing up breakfast, cooking lunch, eating cold new potatoes and making out wedding lists.

'Hullo,' she said, beaming. 'Did you sleep well?'

'Brilliantly,' I said. 'It must be all that fresh air.'

'Don't the church bells sound lovely?' she said, 'I adore country churches—all that soft brick, and sermons about crops, and rosy-cheeked choirboys scuttling in late.'

'Because the vicar's been pinching them in the vestry. It'd be worth going to church to get cool. It's like a sauna on board.'

Gussie looked a bit shocked.

'I don't believe in God,' I said lightly. 'Or rather I've never had any evidence that He believed in me.'

'I didn't think about Him that much,' said Gussie, 'until I found Jeremy, and then I just felt I ought to be saying thank you for my incredible luck all the time.' She bent over to empty the sink tidy, displaying a vast stretch of blue-jeaned bottom. Wranglers must sew up their trousers with underground cables to stand that kind of strain.

'I hoped Jeremy'd wake up in time to go to Matins with me,' she went on, 'but he's still out like a light. Mind you, it's good for him. He's been working so hard at the office, and I often think the strain of getting married is even worse for men.'

She glanced at her list again, absentmindedly breaking off a bit of celery and putting it in her mouth.

'Do you think I'll need a Mac in my trousseau?'

'Well, I've always preferred men with cars,' I said. 'But I suppose you could wear a black plastic one with nothing underneath for the bedroom. Do you need any help?' I added, unenthusiastically, taking an orange from the fruit bowl.

'Oh no,' she said, 'I want you to enjoy yourself.'

'I'll go and sunbathe then.'

I took a lilo and my incredibly boring biography of Matthew Arnold out on deck. I had put on a new black bikini, composed only of four black triangles, held together by bootlaces, with not really enough triangle to go round. The sun was already high in the sky and boring down on the boat. Snaky brown tree roots gleamed below the surface of the oily water. Meadowsweet was spread thick as cream on the lush green banks. The birds were still being shouted down by the church bells. It was far too hot for clothes. I took off my bikini top and lay down. Within twenty minutes sweat was pouring in rivulets down the ridges of the lilo. I was just about to retreat inside for a towel and a drink of water when I heard a wolf whistle. I flicked open my eyes, straight into the highly unacceptable face of capitalism, and quickly flicked them shut again. It was Gareth—already after two days tanned dark brown by the sun—carrying the Sunday papers, a large gin and tonic, and a wireless playing Mozart.

'Morning, lovely,' he said. 'You're overdressed. Why don't you take off the bottom half as well?'

I ignored him, feigning sleep.

The next moment Gussie joined us.

'Oh Tavy,' she said. 'Do you think you should? Someone might see you from the bank.'

'Don't be a spoilsport,' said Gareth. 'Here's the *News of the World*, and shut up. I won't give you a paper, Octavia, as I know you're finding that biography of Matthew Arnold quite unputdownable. Bags I borrow it next.'

I gritted my teeth. For a few minutes they read in silence. I got hotter and hotter, like a chicken on a spit.

'Why do they always write about the emphasis being on the hips this year, when one's just had a huge breakfast?' sighed Gussie.

'That's nice,' said Gareth, showing her *The Sunday Times*. 'They've given us a good write-up, recommending their readers to buy our shares, which is more than they're doing for Seaford-Brennen.'

'How many people work at Seaford-Brennen, Tavy?' said Gussie.

'About a quarter of them,' said Gareth, taking a huge swig at his gin and tonic.

Gussie giggled.

'You don't know anything about them,' I hissed at him. 'Why don't you stick to underpasses, which you seem to know all about?'

'There's a most interesting thing here about schism in the

Catholic church,' said Gussie, hastily. 'Do you think priests should marry, Gareth?'

'Only if they love each other.'

Gussie shrieked with laughter.

There was only one single bell tolling now, hurrying people to church.

'They always ring out of tune back home in Wales,' said Gareth. 'One of the bellringers is a very pretty girl given to wearing mini skirts. All the men bellringers are in love with her, and every time she lets her bell go up, they pull their bells down to have a good look. Christ it's hot. It must be in the nineties.'

'I'm going to get a drink. Do you want one, Tavy?' said Gussie.

'I do,' said Gareth, handing her his glass.

'I hope Jeremy wakes up soon. It'll be much cooler once we get going,' said Gussie.

I turned over on my side, pretending to be asleep. Through the rails I could see the elm trees full of a blue darkness, and a heat haze shimmering above the hay fields. I must have dozed off, for the next thing I heard was Jeremy's voice saying, 'What the hell did you give me last night?'

'Mogodon,' said Gareth.

'Mogodon!' said Jeremy in horror. 'Three of them! Christ, you bastard! That's almost an overdose. No wonder they knocked me out like a sledge hammer.'

'It was for your own good,' said Gareth. 'Kept you out of mischief and Miss Brennen's bed.'

'I wish you'd bloody well stop playing Anti-Cupid,' snapped Jeremy.

'Hush,' said Gareth softly, 'you'll wake Octavia.' Jeremy lowered his voice, 'God she looks fantastic.'

'Like a Ming vase,' said Gareth. 'Beautiful, but empty. Why don't you write one of your famous poems about her? "Oh lovely Octavia, How I'd like to make a slave of ya." '

'Oh, put a sock in it,' said Jeremy angrily.

'Have you got a copy of Shakespeare on board?' asked Gareth.

70

'Somewhere in the bookcase in the saloon. What do you want to look up?'

'*The Taming of the Shrew*,' said Gareth, 'I thought I might pick up a few tips on how to handle Octavia.'

Jeremy lost his temper. 'Will you stop jumping on that poor girl?'

'Why, are you jumping on her already?'

'I am *not*. Why the hell don't you go and start the boat?'

'Why don't you?' said Gareth. 'I've come here on holiday. It's the first break I've had in months, and I'm enjoying the view far too much. I can't decide if Octavia's glorious knockers remind me more of the Himalayas or the Pyramids.'

'Jeremy,' called Gussie—she obviously didn't like Jeremy admiring the view either—'do come and start the boat.'

'All right,' he said, reluctantly; then more softly to Gareth, 'if you don't get off Octavia's back, there'll be trouble.'

'Her back is not the part of her anatomy uppermost in my mind at the moment.'

I was nearly expiring with heat and rage by now. I was also worried about my tits burning. My hair was ringing with sweat. I shook it out of my eyes and glared at Gareth.

'Do you want me to oil you?' he said.

'No thank you,' I hissed.

'Why don't we have a cease-fire. It is the sabbath after all?' he said, looking down at me with amused and lascivious pleasure.

'You're disgusting,' I said, furiously turning over on my front.

There was the sound of engines, and the boat started. Even when we were on the move the heat didn't let up. As we sailed into a long stretch of open river with no shade, Gareth got to his feet and stretched.

'I'm worried you'll overcook, Octavia.'

And the next moment he'd dived into the river with a huge splash, sending a tidal wave of filthy oily water all over me. I leapt up, screaming, grabbing my bikini top.

'Will you stop hounding me,' I howled as he surfaced,

laughing, shaking his hair out of his eyes.

'I thought you needed cooling down,' he said, and, scooping a great handful of water in my direction, soaked me again.

Gibbering with rage, I rushed into the kitchen.

'That sod's just drenched me.'

Gussie giggled. 'Oh poor Tavy! Here, have a towel.'

'It's soaked my hair,' I stormed, 'I must wash it at once.'

'You can't really,' said Gussie, sympathetically. 'There simply isn't enough water. I'm sure it'll dry all right.'

I caught sight of my face in the mirror. There was a great red mark on my cheek where I'd lain on Matthew Arnold. It looked as though Gareth had socked me one, and doubled my ill temper.

'But normally I wash my hair every day,' I screamed. 'It's crawling off my head. I've never been on anything as primitive as this bloody boat.'

Then I made the most awful scene. None of Gussie's bromides could soothe me.

'No one goes out of their way deliberately to hurt people,' she said finally.

'I do,' said Gareth, coming in dripping river water and seizing the towel from me. 'I'm like a leopard, I kill for the hell of it.'

'You shouldn't have soaked her,' said Gussie, reproachfully.

'I'm going back to London,' I said.

'Spendid,' said Gareth. 'There's a fast train on the hour from Reading. Next time you come down we'll arrange QE2 facilities.'

'What's the matter?' said Jeremy, shouting down the stairs.

'We've got a mutiny on our hands, Mr. Christian,' said Gareth, 'Able seawoman Brennen wants to desert. Shall we keelhaul her or give her 1000 lashes?'

Gussie—God rot her—started to laugh.

Jeremy came down the stairs and took in the situation in a swift glance.

'Go and steer,' he said angrily to Gareth. 'You've caused

enough trouble for one morning. I own this boat, and what I say goes.'

'Sorry Captain Bligh, I mistook you for Mr. Christian,' said Gareth, grinning and filling up his glass, he disappeared up the stairs, shouting, 'Ahoy, Ahoy, my kingdom for a hoy.'

Jeremy poured me a stiff drink, and took me into the saloon.

'I'm sorry about Gareth,' he said, gently, 'he's being diabolical. I think he must be going through the change of life.'

'He's probably irritated I haven't succumbed yet,' I said. 'Hell knows no fury like a Welshman scorned.'

There was a pause. Jeremy put some books back on the shelf.

'Did you wait very long last night?' he said in an undertone.

'Not very,' I said. 'I was disappointed, that's all.'

'Oh Christ,' he said. 'Gussie was yapping and yapping away about soft furnishings and the next thing I knew it was morning. Bloody sleeping pills. I'm terribly sorry, you must think me such a drip.'

I laughed, suddenly I felt much happier.

'You couldn't do much on three Mogodons.'

'If you're really desperate for a bath,' he said, 'we'll stop at the next lock and see what we can do.'

'Where are we anyway?' I said.

'About half a mile from Grayston.'

'That's where Ricky Seaford lives,' I said in excitement. 'I'll give him a ring at the next lock and we can go and swim in his pool.'

'I'll come ashore with you,' said Jeremy.

'Behave yourself, Octavia,' Gareth shouted after us as we got off the boat, 'or we'll get The Rape of the Lock Keeper, and Jeremy'll be forced to write a long poem about it afterwards, in heroic couplets.'

Scarlet geraniums blazed in pots on the window-ledges; the whitewashed stone of the lock-keeper's cottage assaulted the eye. The quay scorched my bare feet. Inside the cottage it was dark and at least cooler. Jeremy tactfully stayed outside while I telephoned. The butler answered. Mrs. Seaford was not back from church, but Mr. Seaford was in, he said. That was a relief.

Ricky was a long time coming to the telephone. I watched the flypaper hanging from the ceiling, black with desperate, writhing insects, and examined the coronation mugs and framed photographs of children with white bows in their hair on a nearby dresser.

'Hullo Octavia,' said Ricky's familiar, plummy, port-soaked voice. It sounded more guarded than usual. 'What can I do for you?'

'I'm only a quarter of a mile away,' I said. 'Roughing it on a barge.'

'I can't imagine you roughing it anywhere.'

'Can we come and see you this afternoon?'

There was a pause. I could imagine his bull-terrier eyes narrowing thoughtfully. He probably had business friends staying the weekend. It would impress them to invite a sexy bit of crumpet like myself over but would it be worth incurring Joan's wrath?

Then he said, 'We're going out to dinner, but come over and have tea or early drinks or whatever. Who's on the boat with you?'

'Oh, a sweet engaged couple, you'll absolutely adore them, and a ghastly jumped-up Welshman, who's convinced he's Charlie Clore. I wanted to show him a real Captain of Industry in the flesh. That's why I rang you.'

Ricky laughed. I could tell he was flattered.

'Do put him down if you get the chance,' I said.

'Talking of Captains of Industry,' said Ricky, 'there's a great fan of yours staying here this weekend.'

'Oh, who?'

'Wait and see. We'll see you later.'

Things were decidedly looking up. Gareth and Jeremy were already at each other's throats, and this afternoon I would not only have the pleasure of seeing Ricky take Gareth down a few pegs, but also have an old admirer to spur Jeremy on to greater endeavour. Smiling to myself, I went out into the sunshine.

Jeremy was leaning over the back-door gate, gazing moodily at the sweltering horizon. Above a pair of much faded pale blue denim shorts, his back was tanned a gleaming butterscotch gold. Suddenly I thought what ravishing children we'd have. No one could see us from the boat. I put a hand on his shoulder.

'Stop all-in wrestling with your conscience,' I said. 'It's too hot.'

The next moment I was in his arms.

After a second I pulled away.

'Didn't you know it was dangerous to exceed the stated dose?' I whispered, gazing blatantly at his mouth.

By the time we got back, Gareth had taken the boat through the lock.

'You *have* caught the sun,' said Gussie, gazing at me in admiration. She was obviously pleased I was in a good mood again.

'What's worrying me,' said Gareth, grimly, 'is whose son she's caught.'

9

Great fans of overhanging willow trees crashed against the roof as we drew up at Ricky Seaford's newly painted blue and white boathouse. Hayfields rose pale and silver towards a dark clump of beech trees, surrounding a large russet house, which was flanked by stables, sweeping lawns, and well kept fruit and vegetable gardens.

'Goodness, how glamorous,' said Gussie, standing on the shore and tugging a comb through her tangled hair. 'I hope we don't look too scruffy.'

I certainly didn't. I was wearing a pale pink shirt over my black bikini, and the heat had brought a pink glow to the sun-tan in my cheeks.

'Ricky Seaford's a frightfully big noise, isn't he?' said Gussie.

'Well, he makes a lot of noise,' I said, admiring my reflection in the boathouse window.

'It'll be so useful for Gareth to meet him,' said Gussie.

'Oh he's right out of Gareth's league.'

'Never mind,' said Gareth equably. 'I may pick up a few tips.'

We walked up the slope, past hedges dense and creamy with elder flowers and hogweed. Under huge flat-bottomed trees, sleek horses switched their tails deep in the buttercups. We came to a stile. Jeremy went over first, and helped Gussie and then me. For a second I let myself rest in his arms.

We let ourselves in through a wrought iron gate, walking across unblemished green lawns, past huge herbaceous borders luxuriating in the heat.

'These are Joan's pride and joy,' I said. 'She's very good in flower bed.'

'Is she nice?' said Gussie.

'Well, let's say I prefer Ricky. She's a perfectly bloody mother-in-law to poor Xander.'

At that moment, several assorted gun dogs and terriers poured, barking, out of the French windows, followed at a leisurely pace by Ricky Seaford. He was a tall man, who had grown much better looking in middle age, when his hair had turned from a muddy brown to a uniform silver grey. This suited his rather florid complexion which had been heightened, year by year, by repeated exposure to equal quantities of golf-course air and good whisky. Beneath the bull-terrier eyes the nose was straight, the mouth firm. A dark blue shirt, worn out-side his trousers concealed a middle-aged spread. The general effect was pro-consular and impressive.

'Hullo, chaps,' he said in his booming voice, kissing me on the cheek. 'Joan's down at the pool.' He was always more friendly to me when she was out of earshot.

'This is Gussie Forbes and Jeremy West,' I said.

'Nice to see you,' said Ricky, giving them the big on-off smile that gave him such a reputation for having charm in the city. 'You've certainly picked the right weather.'

Suddenly he saw Gareth who had lingered behind to talk to the dogs. For a minute Ricky looked incredulous, then his face lit up like a Christmas tree.

'Why Gareth,' he bellowed. 'You do pop up in the most unexpected places. What the hell are you doing here?'

'Cruising down the river on a Sunday afternoon,' said Gareth. 'I must say it's a nice place you've got here, Ricky.'

'Well, well, well, I didn't realize you were going to see it so soon.'

Ricky now seemed terribly pleased with everything. 'Fancy you meeting up with this lot. Now I expect you'd like a drink. Come down to the pool. Joan's been so looking forward to meeting you.'

'You know each other?' said Gussie, looking delighted. 'What a coincidence; you never said so, Gareth.'

'No one asked me,' he said.

'Is this all of you?' said Ricky. 'I thought you mentioned some tiresome little parvenu who needed putting in his place, Octavia?'

'That was probably me,' said Gareth drily.

If I'd had a knife handy, I'd certainly have plunged it into him. I moved away, kicking a defenceless-looking petunia when no one was looking.

The pool, which was of Olympic size and always kept at 75 degrees, lay in an old walled garden, overgrown with clematis, ancient pink roses and swathes of honeysuckle. At one end, in a summerhouse, Ricky had built a bar. Joan Seaford, a 15 stone do-gooder, most of it muscle, lay under a green and white striped umbrella, writing letters. She glanced up coldly as we approached. She always looks at me as though I was a washing machine that had broken down. As is often the case, the people who married into the Seaford-Brennen clan were the ones who felt the family rivalry most strongly. The violent jealousy Joan

77

had always displayed towards my mother was now transferred to me and intensified by the resentment she felt towards Xander.

'Hullo Octavia,' she said. 'You're looking very fit.'

Her voice had that carrying quality developed by years of strenuous exercise bawling out gundogs, and terrorizing charity committees. Drawing close I could see the talcum powder caked between her huge breasts, and smell the Tweed cologne she always used.

I introduced Gussie and Jeremy. Ricky had dropped behind, showing the new diving boards to Gareth.

'I've never seen such a beautiful pool,' raved Gussie. 'And your herbaceous borders are out of this world. How on earth do you grow flowers like that? My fiancé and I have just got a house with a tiny garden. We're so excited.'

Joan looked slightly more amiable; her face completely defrosted when Ricky came up and said, 'Darling, isn't this extraordinary? Guess who's on the boat with them—Gareth Llewellyn.'

'Oh, I've heard so much about you.'

'And Octavia's been telling us lots about you, Mrs. Seaford,' said Gareth, taking her hand.

Joan shot me a venomous look, then turned, smiling, back to Gareth.

'My dear, you must call me Joan. I gather you and Ricky have been doing a lot of business together.'

'Well, yes,' said Gareth, the lousy sycophant, still holding her hand. 'We hope to. I must say you've done this pool beautifully.'

'Well what's everyone going to have to drink?' said Ricky, rubbing his hands.

Gussie was putting an awful flowered teacosy on her head.

'I'd love to have a swim first,' she said.

I sat down on the edge of the pool. One of the Seaford setters, sensing my ill-humour, wandered, panting, over to me and shoved a cold nose in my hand. The dogs had always been the only nice people in the house.

My temper had not improved half an hour later. Everyone had swum and Gareth, having totally captivated Joan Seaford, had been taken off to the house to talk business with Ricky. Ricky, having learnt from Gareth that Jeremy was in publishing, had invited him to inspect the library which dripped with priceless first editions that no one had ever read. Gussie was still gambolling round in the shallow end like a pink hippo, rescuing ladybirds from drowning. I was left with Joan.

'Where's Pamela?' I said.

'She's gone off to lunch with some friends—the Connolly-Hockings. He's prospective candidate for Grayston. Xander finds them boring. We were rather surprised he couldn't make it this weekend. You'd think after three weeks in the Far . . .'

'He was exhausted by the trip,' I said. 'It's his first weekend home. I expect he had a lot of things to catch up on.'

'Ricky thought it rather odd he used pressure of work as an excuse,' said Joan. 'He must confine all his industry to the weekends.'

'What do you mean?' I said sharply.

Joan wrote the address of some Viscountess on the envelope in her controlled, schoolgirl hand. Then she said, 'Xander doesn't seem to understand that office hours run more or less from 9.30 to 5.30 with one hour for lunch. He shouldn't spend quite so long every day pouring drinks down young men who ought to be back in their offices at the Stock Exchange.'

Despite the white heat of the day I suddenly felt as though ice cold water was being dripped down my neck. Had Ricky and Joan got wind of Xander's proclivities? God help him if they had.

'Xander does most of his deals over lunchtime drinks,' I protested.

At that moment Gussie joined us.

'Are you talking about Xander?' she said, ripping off her petalled tea cosy. 'I always did think he was the most glamorous man ever—after Jeremy that is.'

Joan gave a wintry smile.

'I gather from Tavy that Pamela is divine too,' said Gareth, having gathered no such thing. 'But I can't believe you've got married daughters, you look so young.'

Joan patted her sculptured blue curls. 'I'm going to be a grandmother soon.'

'How exciting,' shrieked Gussie. 'You didn't tell me Xander was having a baby, Tavy.'

'No, my other daughter,' said Joan. 'She only got married in March, but they don't believe in waiting, unlike Xander and Pammie who've been married two years.'

'Oh that's not long,' said Gussie, soothingly. 'I know she'll get pregnant soon.'

'She might,' said Joan, 'if Xander spent more time at home.'

I flushed and was about to contradict her, when Gussie said, 'Alison was only married in March? Then you must be an expert on weddings. I bet it was lovely.'

'It was rather a success. Poor Ricky had to sell a farm to pay for it. Perhaps you saw the photographs in *The Tatler*?'

'I believe I did,' lied Gussie.

And they were off: Searcy's, The General Trading Company, Peter Jones, soft furnishings and duvets, and cast iron casseroles, and 'weren't lots of little bridesmaids in Laura Ashley dresses much sweeter than grown up ones'. Gussie really ought to cut a disc.

'Alison's husband, Peter, is an absolute charmer,' Joan was saying, 'we like him awfully. They spent their honeymoon in the Seychelles.'

The bitch! God how I wanted to hold her underneath her horrible, chlorinated, aquamarine water, until her great magenta face turned purple.

I watched the Red Admirals burying their faces in the buddleia. I wished Jeremy would tear himself away from the first editions. A great wave of loneliness swept over me.

'If you're in a hurry for a wedding dress,' said Joan, 'I've got a little woman who can run up things awfully quickly. Shall I give her a ring?'

I knew she was only handing out largesse to Gussie like nuts at Christmas to emphasize her disapproval of me.

'Would you mind if I washed my hair, Joan?' I said, getting to my feet. 'I've brought my own shampoo.'

'Of course not; help yourself. Use my bedroom; there are plenty of towels in the hot cupboard.'

And arsenic in the taps, I muttered, walking towards the house, feeling her hatred boring into my back. She was probably glad of an excuse to question Gussie about me and Gareth. As I crossed the lawn I deliberately didn't look into the library to see if I could see Jeremy.

Suddenly a voice with a slight foreign accent said, 'Hullo, Octavia.'

I gave a shudder of revulsion as I looked up into the coarse, sensual face of Andreas Katz, porn-king and multimillionaire.

'What are you doing here?' I said, not bothering to keep the hostility out of my voice.

'Staying here.'

So this was the old admirer Ricky was talking about.

'Let me monopolize you for a minute,' he said, taking my arm. I felt his fingers, warm and sweaty, enveloping it. I moved away, but his grip tightened.

'Come and look at Joan's rose-garden,' he said. 'I gather it's quite exceptional.'

I could see the line on his forehead where the man-tan ended and the gunmetal grey hair began. He was a man who seldom ventured out of doors. His eyes were so dark the pupils were indistinguishable from the iris, and always looked so deeply and knowingly into mine, I felt he knew exactly the colour my pants were. He was wearing a black shirt and silver paisley scarf which blended perfectly with the gunmetal hair. I supposed he was handsome in a brutal, self-conscious way, but I could never look at him without realizing what a really evil man he was. I was surprised Joan allowed him into the house. Inflation makes strange bedfellows.

As well as owning strip clubs and half the girly magazines in London, he also produced a prestigious semi-pornographic magazine called *Hedonist* which ran features by intellectuals alongside photographs of naked girls with Red Indian suntans lying on fur counterpanes. It was regarded as the English answer to *Playboy*. For a number of years now he had been chasing me in a leisurely fashion, offering me larger and larger sums to be photographed. I always refused him. I didn't fancy a staple through my midriff. I felt towards him that contempt with which one regards a bath rail in an hotel bathroom, convinced one will never be old and frail enough to need it.

I stopped to admire a purple rose. Andreas admired my figure, which, in its sopping wet bikini, left nothing to the imagination.

He pressed a clenched fist gently against my stomach.

'When are you going to come and pose for me?' he asked.

'I'm not. I don't need the bread.'

'You never know,' he said. 'Nothing's guilt-edged any more. Not even your beautiful hair. Roots cost money to be touched up.'

'It's natural,' I snapped.

'I hear Seaford-Brennen's are in a spot of bother,' he went on. I could feel his hot breath on my shoulder.

'Oh for God's sake, why does everyone keep telling me this? Of course they're all right. They've been all right for over fifty years.'

Andreas splayed his fingers out and caressed my rib cage. He was the only man I knew who gave me that horrible squirming feeling of excitement. I imagined the hundreds of girls and the millions of grubby girly pictures those fingers had flicked through. I moved off sharply and buried my face in a dark red rose. He lit a cigar with a beautiful manicured hand, holding it between finger and thumb like a workman. I could feel him watching me.

'Why don't you stop staring?'

'A Katz can look at a Queen.' He'd made that joke a hundred times before. 'You're a very beautiful girl, Octavia, but not a very bright one. I'll pay you fifteen hundred for one photographic session. Why don't we have dinner next week and discuss it? And that wouldn't be the end, you know. I could give you everything you want.'

'Well, I certainly don't want you,' I said, turning and walking back. 'And if people saw the goods displayed so blatantly across your gatefold, they might not be interested in purchasing them any more.'

Andreas smiled the knowing smile of a crafty old animal.

'I'll get you in the end, baby, and by then it'll be on my terms. You wait and see. By the way, what's Gareth Llewellyn doing closeted with Ricky?'

'He's spending the weekend with us on the boat.'

Andreas laughed. 'So he's your latest. No wonder you're not interested in bread at the moment.'

I looked towards the house, the wistaria above the library was nearly over and shedding its petals in an amethyst carpet over the lawn. Out of the library window I caught sight of Jeremy watching us. I turned and smiled warmly at Andreas.

'There's a beautiful girl down at the pool, talking to Joan. Why don't you go and sign her up instead of me?' I said and, patting him on the cheek, ran laughing into the house.

Joan Seaford must have got the most sexless bedroom in the world, with its *eau de nil* walls, sea green carpet, and utterly smooth flowered counterpane tucked neatly under the pillows so they lay like a great sausage across the top of the bed. On the chest of drawers stood large framed Lenare photographs of Pamela and Alison, looking mistily glamorous in pearls. There were also a large photograph of Peter, Alison's husband, and one of Alison and Peter on their wedding day, knee deep in little bridesmaids in Laura Ashley dresses, but not even a passport snap of Xander, who was a hundred times more handsome than the whole lot put together. I was tempted to take the picture of him out of my wallet and stick it on top of Peter's smug, smiling, square-jawed face, but it wouldn't have done Xander any good.

I felt better after I'd had a bath, washed my hair and rubbed quantities of Joan's bottle of Joy over my body. I hoped she wouldn't recognize the smell on me. Anyway, she deserved to be Joyless, the old bag.

Combing my wet hair, I looked out of the window. Two

girls—the kind who open their legs like airport doors whenever a man approaches—wearing white bikinis, stiletto heels and about a hundredweight each of make-up, were teetering across the lawn. They must have been brought down by Andreas. He always carried a spare. Suddenly Jeremy came out of the door leading to the swimming pool and walked past the tarts without even noticing them. They, on the other hand, swivelled round, gazing at him in wonder, watching him avidly as he loped with lazy animal grace towards the house. I can't say I blamed them.

Bring me my beau of burning gold, I muttered, as, wrapped only in a huge fluffy blue towel, I curled up on the floor to dry my hair. I didn't wait long. There was a quick step outside, and a knock on the door.

'Come in,' I said huskily.

He closed the door behind him. I let the towel slip slightly.

'Why are you here?' I said. 'I'm amazed you could tear yourself away from those first editions.'

'You're why I'm here,' he said. 'Who was that repulsive man you were talking to?'

My heart sang. It had worked.

'Andreas Katz. I've known him for years.'

'How well?'

I went on drying my hair.

'How well?' persisted Jeremy. 'Oh for God's sake, turn that bloody thing off.'

'Not as well as he would like,' I said, but I turned off the dryer.

He put his hands down, pulled me to my feet and kissed me passionately, his hands moving down to my breasts and over my hips. Just for once, I thought, the millpond smoothness of Joan's flowered counterpane is going to be ruffled. Then suddenly Jeremy pushed me away and went over to the window.

It took him a few seconds to get himself under control. I picked up the dryer.

'No,' he said. 'For Christ's sake don't turn it on yet. Look, you must understand how crazy I am about you.'

84

'You've got a funny way of showing it.'

He knelt down beside me, took my face in his hands, began stroking it very gently, as though he wanted to memorize all the contours.

'Gus doesn't deserve to be hurt, you know that as well as I do. Not now anyway, when Gareth's around to fuck everything up as well. If you and I have got something going for us, and I believe we have, let's wait until we get back to London.'

For a minute I looked mutinous. But I knew it wouldn't further my cause to tell him that part of the charm of hooking him would be to upset Gussie and Gareth.

'It's only tonight and Monday to get through,' he went on. 'On Tuesday we go back to London and we can meet on Wednesday and decide what the hell to do about it. You're so important to me, I reckon it's worth waiting for.'

I nodded, picking up his hand and planting a kiss in the palm. 'All right, I'll try,' I said.

With the tips of his fingers he traced a vein on the inside of my arm, down to the scar that ran across my wrist.

'How did you get that?'

'With a razor. The day Xander married Pamela. I felt the only person in the world who really loved me was being taken away from me.'

He bent his head and kissed the scar.

'You do need looking after, don't you? Be brave and trust me, little one. It isn't long to wait.'

After he was gone I finished drying my hair, and went downstairs, experiencing a great and joyous calm. The road was clear now, there was nothing Gareth could do.

Down at the pool the two tarts were swimming, holding their made-up faces high out of the water, encouraged by Gareth, who was sitting on the edge talking to Ricky and Andreas, and drinking a Bloody Mary. He'd been swimming again and his black hair fell in wet tendrils on his forehead.

'I certainly don't want yes-men around me anymore,' said Ricky.

'I certainly want "yes" women around me,' said Gareth. 'I suppose we'd better go in a minute. Oh, there you are Octavia, cleansed in mind and body I hope.'

The three men looked at me. Together they made a nerve-racking trio.

'Octavia has so far refused to cook a single meal on board,' said Gareth. 'So no doubt I'll be slaving over a hot tin opener again tonight. I really don't approve of role-reversal.'

'The only time any role-reversal takes place in our house,' said Ricky, laughing heartily, 'is when Joan reverses the Rolls into the gateposts.'

'Who's taking my name in vain?' said Joan, coming through the gate, followed by Gussie and Jeremy, absolutely weighed down with loot from the vegetable garden.

'Look,' screamed Gussie. 'Isn't Joan angelic? We can have asparagus for supper tonight, and strawberries.'

'At least we won't get scurvy,' said Gareth, smiling at Joan. 'Thank you very much.' He got up. 'We must go.'

'You'd better go and change darling,' said Ricky. 'I'll walk down to the boathouse with them. It'll give the dogs a run. I won't be long.'

He bustled into the house.

'Such a pity we're going out to supper,' Joan said, kissing Gussie. 'Do send me a postcard when you know what your telephone number's going to be. And I'll get Alison and Peter to give you a ring. I know you'll get on.'

'Goodbye, Octavia.' She gave me the usual chilly peck.

'You must bring Mrs. Smith down one evening,' she said to Gareth. 'I hear she's the most gorgeous gel.'

She'd only started saying 'gel' since Pamela came out.

Ricky returned with the visitor's book. 'You must all sign before you go.'

He always does this so he can remember who to claim on expenses. I didn't dare look at Jeremy when Gussie signed them both under their new address.

'We won't be actually living there for a month or two,' she said, beaming round.

Andreas abandoned us at the edge of the hayfields. He was not cut out for country walks.

'Goodbye Octavia,' he said. 'Think about what I've said. We can't go on not meeting like this.'

'That man's a shit,' said Gareth, as soon as we were out of earshot.

'I know,' said Ricky, 'but an extremely clever one.'

10

After the thrill of my recent encounter with Jeremy I behaved atrociously for the rest of the day. As we were sailing towards evening through low fields of buttercups and overhanging trees, I made Jeremy teach me how to steer the boat. I insisted on driving it towards the bank all the time, so he had to keep putting his hands over mine in order to straighten up. Gussie seemed to see nothing wrong. She beamed at us both. Gareth was making Pimms.

After dinner Gussie dragged a very reluctant Jeremy across the fields to look at a Norman church, and Gareth and I were left on the boat together drinking brandy. The night was very hot and still. An owl hooted in a nearby spinney. The first star flickered like a white moth in a dark blue sky. Gareth smoked a cigar to keep off the midges. The wireless was playing Beethoven's Third Piano Concerto. If only it was Jeremy sitting there, I thought. Nevertheless, I'd made such good progress that day. I felt nothing could dim my happiness.

Gareth got up, flicked his cigar into the water and strolled over to the other side of the boat to stand looking at the darkening horizon.

'How's your weekend of sun, sex and sleep going?' I asked.

'Not quite as eventfully as yours,' he said.

He came and stood over me, looking down at me, huge against the sky. Suddenly my heart began to thump unpleasantly, perhaps at last he was going to try his luck with me after all.

'I want another drink,' I said, getting quickly to my feet and wandering into the saloon.

Gareth followed me. 'Aren't you beginning to wonder why I haven't made a pass at you?'

I turned round. 'Since you seem quite incapable of passing anyone up, it had crossed my mind.'

He looked at me for a minute and then grinned.

'Because I don't like bitches, and you're the biggest bitch I've ever met.'

Wham! I let him have it, slap across the cheek. He didn't flinch, he didn't even put his hand up to his face.

'And that seems to substantiate my theory,' he said, pulling a packet of cigarettes out of his hip pocket and offering me one. I shook my head dumbly, appalled at what I had done. He selected a cigarette carefully and then lit it.

'You're not really my type,' he went on. 'I like my women gentle and loving, soft and tender. Women so vulnerable I want to protect them just as I'd look after a kitten or a little girl lost in the street. Women who don't automatically expect me to love them more than they love me. Maybe once upon a time before everyone started spoiling you you were like that, but not any more. You're so hard now, lovely, they could cut a diamond on you.'

'How dare you speak to me like that!' I said furiously.

'Because I'm probably the first man you've ever met who's been left completely cold by you. I've met your sort before; you're just a prick teaser or what the French call an "*allumeuse*", more anxious to inflame men than gratify them once they're well and truly hooked. You give off so much promise with that marvellous body and that great bright mane of hair falling over your eyes. And you've got the most beautiful face

88

I've ever seen. But it doesn't add up to a thing, because you're so much in love with yourself that there isn't room for anyone else.'

'Shut up,' I said in a choked voice. 'I don't want to listen.'

'And another thing,' he went on, pouring a couple of fingers of brandy into his glass, 'although you've probably seen more ceilings than Michaelangelo, I guess you've never got any pleasure out of all those men you've slept with, and that troubles you a bit, because you've read somewhere that sex is supposed to be rather enjoyable and you can't understand why it doesn't work for you.'

It was like a nightmare.

'Stop it, stop it!' I screamed. 'You don't understand anything. I was going to get married but he was killed in a car crash only a few months ago.'

'I know all about that,' he said softly. 'Tod was never going to marry you.'

I clutched the table for support; my legs seemed to give way.

'You knew him?' I whispered. 'I don't understand. Then you knew . . .'

'. . . All about you long before I met you?' said Gareth. 'Yes, of course I did. Tod was living with an old girl friend of mine, Cathie Summers. They were fantastic together until you came along and broke it up.'

'I didn't break it up,' I whispered.

'Oh yes you did, lovely. You waited until Cathie'd gone to the States for a week and then you moved in. But it wasn't any good. Tod was fallible like most men, but he saw through you pretty quickly.'

'You're wrong. You're wrong. He loved me far more than he did her! He was with me the night he was killed.'

Gareth turned to me, his eyes suddenly stony with contempt.

'I know he was. But as usual Miss Brennen—Myth Brennen I ought to call you—you're bending the facts. Tod and I had a drink in the Antelope that night. Cathie was due back the next day, and Tod was in a panic about what she'd say if she found out about you. He was steeling himself to come round and tell you it was all off. I told him not to bother, just to let you stew. But Tod, being an ethical sod, insisted on going through with it.'

'That's right,' I stammered. 'And the moment he saw me he realized it was me he loved, not Cathie, and he was going to give her up.'

'You're a bloody liar,' said Gareth. 'Tod left me in the pub at five to eleven. He must have been with you by eleven o'clock. He was killed at ten past eleven—driving like the devil to get away from you.'

For a second I couldn't move or tear my eyes away from his. Then I gave a sob and fled out of the saloon down the passage to my cabin and, throwing myself down on my bunk, broke into a storm of weeping. I couldn't stand it. Gareth knew Tod, he knew all about me. He'd looked into my mind and seen everything—the aridity, the desert, the emptiness—and he'd brought to light terrible things I'd never admitted, even to myself, disproving lies that even I had begun to believe were the truth. I cried and cried, great tearing sobs until I thought there were no more tears inside me, then I just lay there, my face buried in my sodden pillow, trembling with terror.

Much later I heard Jeremy and Gussie come back. Oh God, I thought in agony, I expect Gareth's giving them a blow-by-blow account of the whole incident. They must have stayed up to watch the midnight movie, because it was half-past two before Gareth came to bed.

'Octavia,' he said softly.

I didn't answer. I ached for Jeremy. I wanted him to take me in his arms, to caress and console me and reconcile me with myself.

I didn't sleep all night. Great waves of anguish kept sweeping over me. I toyed with the idea of creeping off the boat before anyone was up and going back to London. But how would I get there? There wasn't a railway station for miles. I suppose I could ring one of my boyfriends and ask them to drive down and collect me. But would they? I'd never doubted I could get a man back at the drop of a hat. Now, suddenly, I wasn't sure.

I was feeling so paranoid I could hardly get myself out of bed. Thank God I'd brought the biggest pair of dark glasses in the world with me. In the kitchen Jeremy and Gussie were cooking breakfast.

'If you've got a hangover like the rest of us,' said Gussie, 'there's some Alka Seltzer in the cupboard.'

'No, I haven't actually.' Gussie poured me out a cup of coffee.

'Do you take sugar?'

'Of course she doesn't, she's quite sweet enough as it is,' said Jeremy, smiling at me. He was so used to getting the come-on sign from me, he seemed amazed I didn't crack back, and when he handed me my cup, his fingers closed over mine for a second. Yesterday I would have been certain he was trying to make contact with me; now my self-confidence had taken such a bashing, I felt it must be accidental.

I took my coffee up on deck. Three vast pairs of pants and the biggest bra in the Western Hemisphere were dripping from the railing. Gussie had obviously been doing some washing. A silver haze lay over the countryside. Pale green trees rose tender as lovers from the opposite bank. I couldn't stop shaking. Amidst all this beauty and sunshine, I felt like an empty shell.

A minute later Gussie came and joined me.

'What a beautiful shirt that is,' she said. 'I do envy you, Tavy. It doesn't matter if you've got a hangover or feel off colour, you've got such a lovely figure and such marvellous hair, people still think you're a knock-out. But with me, my face is the only thing I've got—and that isn't all that great—and when that looks awful,'—she squinted at herself in the cabin window—'like today, with this spot, I've got nothing to offer.'

She looked down at her left hand and flashed her engagement ring in the sun.

'Jeremy's wild about you,' she said wistfully. 'He was teasing me yesterday, saying that I was lucky I'd got his ring on my finger before he met you, or heaven knows what would have happened.'

I suddenly wondered what Jeremy was playing at.

'He's got no right to say that,' I said crossly. 'He adores you. You've only got to see the way he looks at you when you don't know he's looking.'

She looked at me, delighted.

'Do you really think so? Oh that does make me feel so much better. You don't think me silly?'

I shook my head and she went on. 'I was convinced Jeremy'd fallen for you. I was really screwed up about it. That's why I've been eating so much lately. Not that I thought for a moment you'd lead him on. I mean, you're one of my best friends—at least you were at school, I hope you still are. But you're so beautiful I didn't see how he could help it. And somehow you look so good together.

'That's why when he suggested asking you down for the weekend, I persuaded him to ask Gareth as well. Gareth's so attractive, I thought you were bound to fancy him and that would put Jeremy off.'

God, how naive she was! I concentrated on lighting a cigarette. Oh why were my hands shaking so much?

'I like Jeremy enormously,' I said slowly. 'He's extremely attractive too, but I also think he's perfect for you.'

'I'm not sure he's perfect for me at all,' said Gussie. 'I think he'll probably be wildly unfaithful to me, but that's because underneath he's not very sure of himself, and he'll need to make passes at women from time to time, just to boost his ego. But I hope so long as I make him happy enough, he'll always come back to me in the end.'

I looked at her round earnest face, appalled.

'But you can't marry him, Gus, not thinking that!'

'Oh yes I can. I love him so much it hurts sometimes. And I know it'll kill me when he is unfaithful, but at least I can try and make him more secure by loving him.'

I looked at her in awe. This was the sort of girl Gareth was talking about last night. Friday's child, loving and giving, prepared to give far more than she took.

Jeremy came up on deck. His blond hair gleamed almost white from the sun. Instinctively I turned my head away.

'I wish Gareth would step on it,' he said.

'Where's he gone?'

'To ring up some friends of his who live a few miles up the river,' said Jeremy. 'He thought we might take a drink off them. He must have run out of 2ps by now.'

'Here he comes,' said Gussie.

Gareth walked up the path, whistling. He grinned when he saw us, wicked gypsy eyes narrowed against the sun. He bounded up the bank and, scorning the gangplank, jumped across onto the boat. He looked up at Gussie's underclothes on the line.

'Is that a signal?' he said. 'England expects every man to do Octavia?'

'Did you get through?' snapped Jeremy.

Gareth nodded. 'We've timed it very well. They're giving a party tonight. They want us all to go. The land at the back of their house slopes straight down to the river. They suggested we tie up there about teatime. Then you two girls can have baths and tart up at your leisure.'

'How super,' said Gussie. 'But I haven't got anything to wear. Will it be very smart?'

'I don't expect so. Anyway they can lend you something if it is.'

I turned away. My palms were damp with sweat. The thought of a party terrified me. Drinks and noise and people I didn't know. They would be Gareth's friends too, probably as tough and flash and sarcastic as Gareth himself. He must have warned them about me already—the tart with the heart of ice.

'We'd better get moving,' said Jeremy. 'I'll start up the engine.'

'I'll wash up,' I said, diving into the kitchen.

No one had washed up last night's plates and, as we were

running short of water, I had to wash everything in the same grey, greasy liquid.

'Hi,' said a voice. Gareth was standing in the doorway. I stiffened and concentrated hard on the bubbles of yellow fat floating on top of the washing-up water.

'Hullo,' I said with studied lightness. I was determined to show him that yesterday's showdown hadn't bothered me in the least.

He came and put his hand on my shoulder. I jumped away as though he'd burnt me.

'Easy now,' he said. 'I only wanted to apologize for last night. Not for what I said, because it needed saying, but I should have put it more tactfully.'

'If you think anything you said last night had any effect on me, you're very much mistaken,' I said in a stifled voice. 'Damn! We're out of Quix.'

With a swift movement he took off my dark glasses.

'Don't! Don't you dare!' I spat at him. I didn't want him to see how red and puffed my eyes were with crying.

'All in good time,' he said. He had me cornered now. God, he was big. His very size in that kitchen was stifling, overpowering. I backed away against the draining board, looking down at my hands, trembling with humiliation.

'Why do you keep bullying me?' I whispered.

I'd done that trick before, letting my breasts rise and fall very fast in simulated emotion, but now I found I couldn't stop myself.

Gareth put his hand under my chin and forced it upwards. For an insane, panicky moment, I wondered whether to bite him, anything to drive him away, to destroy this suffocating nearness. Then he let go of me, and handed me back my dark glasses.

'You can actually look ugly,' he said, in surprise. 'I don't know why, but I find that very encouraging.'

'Gareth,' shouted Jeremy, 'can you come and open the lock gates?'

'Just coming,' Gareth shouted. He turned as he went up the

steps. 'Don't forget it's your turn to put on the chef's hat and cook us lunch.'

That was *all* I needed. I opened the door of the fridge and the baleful eye of a huge chicken peered out at me. How the hell did one cook the beastly thing?

Gussie popped her head through the door.

'Gareth says you're going to cook lunch. How lovely. I'll truss the chicken for you if you like, and then you can make that thing you made us the other night. There's masses of cream and lemon juice in the fridge.'

She'd only just had breakfast and her mouth was watering already.

'Thank you,' I said weakly. Why, oh why, had I been so foolish as to pass Luigi's *haute cuisine* off as my own last week?

I go hot and cold every time I remember that lunch. I got in such a muddle that we didn't eat until three o'clock, by which time the others were absolutely starving. I shall never forget their hungry flushed faces turning gradually to dismay as they sat down to eat and realized the chicken was burnt to a frazzle, the sauce was curdled past redemption and the spinach boiled away to a few gritty stalks. But the potatoes were the worst disaster. Because I hadn't realized you had to roast them longer than twenty minutes, they were hard as bullets.

'It's a pity we haven't got a twelve bore on board,' said Gareth. 'Then we could have spent the afternoon shooting pigeons with them.'

'It's absolutely delicious,' said Gussie, chewing valiantly away at a piece of impossibly dry chicken.

Jeremy said nothing. Gareth laughed himself sick. He didn't even make any attempt to eat, just lit a cigar, blew smoke over everyone, and said at last he understood why Gussie was always going on about the importance of having a good breakfast.

I escaped on deck and sat there gazing at the pink rose petals drifting across the khaki water. The panic and terror of the morning were fast hardening into hatred against Gareth. Once and for all I was going to get even with him.

Jeremy came and sat down beside me.

'What's the matter?' he asked gently.

'Nothing,' I said. 'I get these blinding migraines sometimes, they make me completely stupid. I'm sorry I loused up lunch.'

'Hell, that doesn't matter. We should never have let you do all the cooking. Why didn't you tell us you were feeling awful?'

I smiled up at him. 'It'll go soon. Do we have to go to this party tonight?'

'Of course not, if you don't want to. I rather fancy going, just for the sake of going into a room with you, and everyone thinking you belong to me.'

'You win,' I said.

He took my hand. 'Do you still dislike Gareth that much?'

'Is it that obvious?'

He nodded. 'A bit.'

He caught at a leaf of an overhanging tree. 'Gus gets some funny ideas. She thinks you're very mixed up beneath the panache and the sophistication. She says you need someone like Gareth to sort you out.'

'How kind of Gussie to be so concerned with my welfare,' I said, trying to keep the tremble of anger out of my voice.

There was a burst of laughter from the other end of the boat. Such was my paranoia, I was convinced Gussie and Gareth were talking about me.

'Would you make me any different?' I asked, looking deep into Jeremy's eyes.

'I'd just like to make you,' he said. 'Let's not bother about irrelevancies.'

It's the same old story, I thought, as I did my face before we went ashore. Now he's really pursuing me, I don't want him so much. The intensity and lust in his eyes had me frightened. I had a feeling I might have got a tiger by the tail.

My thoughts turned to Gussie and Gareth.

'Insecure, unhappy, mixed-up, frigid, hard enough to cut a diamond on.' They were having a field-day passing judgements

96

on me. How dare that fat slob Gussie patronize me, how dare Gareth take it upon himself to tell me so many home truths? The chips were down. If they thought I was a bitch, all right, I was going to behave like one.

II

Later in the afternoon as we went across water meadows into a large orchard, we could see a Queen Anne house through the trees.

'What are these people called?' asked Gussie.

'Hamilton,' said Gareth. 'Hesketh and Bridget. They've got hordes of children, but I don't know if any of them are at home.'

Gussie picked a scarlet cherry up from the long grass. 'And they're nice?'

'Nice, but perfectly crazy,' said Gareth. 'Hesketh has madness on one side of the family and a Rumanian grandmother on the other, so you never know what to expect.'

'I bet they're hell,' I whispered to Jeremy.

But they weren't hell. They were a gently unworldly middle-aged couple. Hesketh Hamilton was tall and thin with spectacles on the end of his nose. He had been gardening and was wearing faded blue dungarees and a kind of mauve and white striped baseball cap on his head to keep off the sun. His wife had straggly pepper and salt hair, drawn back into a bun, and eyes the colour of faded denim. She was wearing odd shoes and an old felt skirt covered in dog hairs. They were both obviously delighted to see Gareth.

The house was beautiful but terribly untidy, with books and

97

papers everywhere. It didn't look as though anyone could possibly be giving a party that night. The afternoon sun slanting through the drawing-room window showed thick layers of dust on everything. Assorted dogs lay on the carpet panting from the heat.

'We'll have tea in the garden,' said Bridget Hamilton. 'You can come into the kitchen and help me carry the tray, Gareth. I want you to tell me if Hesketh's got enough drink for this evening. We seem to have asked rather a lot of people.'

Out in the garden the lawn sloped down to a magnificent herbaceous border. Through an iron archway swarming with red roses, deckchairs and a table were set out under a walnut tree.

Gussie as usual went berserk, gushing like an oil well.

'What a fantastic garden! My mother would be green with envy! Look at those roses and those fabulous blue hollyhocks!'

'They're delphiniums,' said Hesketh Hamilton gently.

'Oh yes,' said Gussie unabashed. 'And that heavenly catmint. I love the smell.'

'It always reminds me of oversexed tomcats,' Hesketh said, smiling.

'It's so kind of you to let us all come to your party,' said Gussie, sitting down and putting a very severe strain on a deckchair.

She ought to be re-christened Gushie, I thought savagely.

Gareth came across the lawn carrying a tray, his eyes slanting away from the smoke of his cigar.

'You've got enough drink in, Hesketh, to float the QE2,' he said.

Bridget Hamilton, her hands still covered in earth from gardening, poured black tea into chipped mugs and handed sandwiches round.

'How many of the children are home?' asked Gareth.

'Only Lorna, and she doesn't know you're all coming. She's taken her new horse out. Absolute madness in this heat. She's not such a child now you know, Gareth. She'll be eighteen in August.'

Gareth grinned. 'I know. I hope you've been keeping her on

ice for me.'

He helped himself to a cucumber sandwich as big as a doorstep.

'I'm starving.' He gave an unpleasant smile in my direction. 'I don't know why but I couldn't eat a thing at lunchtime.'

Bridget Hamilton turned to me. 'And what do you do in London? You look like a model or an actress or something.'

'She's quite unemployable,' said Gareth.

Bridget looked reproving. 'I see you're as rude as ever, Gareth.' She smiled at me. 'I never worked in my life until I got married. Anyway, I expect you meet lots of interesting people.'

'Yes I do,' I said.

She sighed. 'The one I'd like to meet is Britt Ekland—so charming looking. Wouldn't you like to meet Britt Ekland, Hesketh?'

'Who's he?' said Hesketh.

Inevitably there was a good deal of laughter at this and Bridget Hamilton was just explaining, 'He's a she, Hesketh, he's a she,' when a door slammed and there was a sound of running footsteps and a girl exploded through the French windows. She was as slim as a blade, in jodhpurs and a red silk shirt, with a mass of curly hair and a freckled, laughing face. Her eyes lighted on Gareth and she gave a squeal of delight.

'Gareth! What are you doing here? How lovely to see you!'

Gareth levered himself out of the deckchair and took both of her hands and stared at her for a long time.

'But you've grown so beautiful, Lorna.'

She flushed. 'Oh Golly, have I really turned into a swan at last?'

'A fully-fledged, paid-up member,' he said, bending forward and kissing her smooth brown cheek. There was not much more he could do with us all watching him, but I had the feeling he wanted to take her into his arms and kiss the life out of her.

'You might acknowledge someone else, darling,' grumbled her mother.

'Oh I'm sorry!' The girl beamed at the rest of us. 'I'm Lorna. It's just that I'm so pleased to see Gareth. You will stay for the party, won't you?' she added anxiously.

'I suppose we ought to think about washing a few glasses and rolling up the carpet,' said Hesketh Hamilton.

'I must wash my hair,' said Bridget. 'It's the only way I'll get the garden out of my nails.'

'Aren't they complete originals?' said Gussie, as she and I changed later. She was wandering around in the nude trying to look at her back. Between her fiery red legs and shoulders, her skin was as white as lard.

'I'm not peeling, am I?' she asked anxiously. 'It itches like mad.'

'Looks a bit angry,' I said, pleased to see that a few tiny white blisters had formed between her shoulders. It'd be coming off her in strips tomorrow.

'Isn't that girl Lorna quite devastating?' she went on. 'You could see Gareth wanted to absolutely gobble her up.'

'She's not that marvellous,' I said, starting to pour water over my hair.

'Oh but she is—quite lovely and so natural. Think of being seventeen again, all the things one was going to do, the books one was going to write, the places one was going to visit. I must say when a girl is beautiful at seventeen she gets a glow about her that old hags like you and I in our twenties can never hope to achieve.'

'Speak for yourself,' I muttered into the washbasin.

I knew when I finally finished doing my face that I'd never looked better. My eyes glittered brilliantly blue in my sun-tanned face; my hair, newly washed and straight, was almost white from the sun. Gussie, I'm glad to say, looked terrible. She was leaning out of the window when there was a crunch of wheels on the gravel outside.

'Oh look, someone's arriving. It's the vicar.'

'We're obviously in for a wild evening,' I said.

'We'd better go down. Shall I wait?'

'No. I'll be ready in a minute. You go on.'

I was glad when she'd gone. I thought she might kick up a fuss at the dress I was going to wear. It was a short tunic in silver chain mail—the holes as big as half-crowns. High-necked at the front, it swooped to positive indecency at the back. Two very inadequate circles of silver sequins covered my breasts. I didn't wear anything underneath except a pair of flesh-coloured pants, which gave the impression I wasn't wearing anything at all.

Slowly I put it on, thinking all the time of the effect it would have on Jeremy when I walked into the sedate country living room. I gave a final brush to my hair and turned to look in the mirror. It was the first time I'd worn it with all my party war-paint, and the impact made even me catch my breath. Oh my, said I to myself, you're going to set them by their country ears tonight. I was determined to make an entrance, so I fiddled with my hair until I could hear that more people had arrived.

There was a hush as I walked into the drawing-room. Everyone gazed at me. Men's hands fluttered up to straighten their ties and smooth their hair, the women stared at me with ill-concealed envy and disapproval.

'Christ!' I heard Jeremy say, in appalled wonder.

But I was looking at Gareth. For the first time I saw a blaze of disapproval in his eyes. I've got under his guard at last, I thought in triumph.

There seemed to be no common denominator among the guests. They consisted of old blimps and tabby cats, several dons from the University, and their ill-dressed wives, a handful of people of Lorna's age, the girls very debbie, the boys very wet, and a crowd of tough hunting types with braying voices and brick red faces. It was as though the Hamiltons had asked everyone they knew and liked, with a total disregard as to whether they'd mix.

I wandered towards Jeremy, Gussie and Gareth.

'I see you've thrown yourself open to the public,' said Gareth, but he didn't smile. 'I suppose I'd better go and hand round some drinks.'

'You shouldn't have worn that dress, Octavia,' said Gussie in a shocked voice. 'This isn't London, you know.'

'That's only too obvious,' I said, looking round.

Bridget Hamilton came over and took my arm. 'How enchanting you look, Octavia. Do come and devastate our local MFH. He's dying to meet you.'

He wasn't the only one. Once those hunting types had had a few drinks, they all closed in on me, vying for my attention. Over and over again I let my glass be filled up. Never had my wit been more malicious or more sparkling. I kept them all in fits of braying laughter.

Like an experienced comedian, although I was keeping my audience happy, I was very conscious of what was going on in the wings—Jeremy, looking like a thundercloud because I was flirting so outrageously with other men, Gareth behaving like the Hamilton's future son-in-law, whether he was coping with drinks or smiling into Lorna's eyes. Every so often, however, his eyes flickered in my direction, and his face hardened.

About ten o'clock, Bridget Hamilton wandered in, very red in the face, and carrying two saucepans, and plonked them down on a long polished table beside a pile of plates and forks.

'There's risotto here,' she said vaguely, 'if anyone's hungry.'

People surged forward to eat. I stayed put, the men around me stayed put as well. The din we were making increased until Gareth pushed his way through the crowd.

'You ought to eat something, Octavia,' he said.

I shook my head and smiled up at him insolently.

'Aren't you hungry?' drawled the MFH who was lounging beside me.

I turned to him, smiling sweetly, 'Only for you.'

A nearby group of women stopped filling their faces with risotto and talking about nappies, and looked at me in horror. The MFH's wife was among them. She had a face like a well-bred cod.

'The young gels of today are not the same as they were twenty years ago,' she said loudly.

'Of course they're not,' I shouted across at her. 'Twenty

years ago I was only six. You must expect some change in my appearance and behaviour.'

She turned puce with anger at the roar of laughter that greeted this. Gareth didn't laugh. He took hold of my arm.

'I think you'd better come and eat,' he said in even tones.

'I've told you once,' I snapped, 'I don't want to eat. I want to dance. Why doesn't someone put on the record player?'

The MFH looked down at the circles of silver sequins.

'What happens to those when you dance?'

I giggled. 'Now you see me, now you don't. They've been known to shift off centre.'

There was another roar of laughter.

'Well, what are we waiting for?' said the MFH. 'Let's put a record on and dance.'

'All right,' I said, looking up at him under my lashes, 'But I must go to the loo first.'

Upstairs in the bathroom, I hardly recognized myself. I looked like some Maenad, my hair tousled, my eyes glittering, my cheeks flushed. God, the dress was so beautiful.

'And you're so beautiful too,' I added and, leaning forward, lightly kissed my reflection in the mirror.

Even in my alcoholic state, I was slightly abashed when I turned round and saw Gareth standing watching me from the doorway.

'Don't you know it's rude to stare?' I said.

He didn't move.

'I'd like to come past—if you don't mind,' I went on.

'Oh no, you don't,' he said, grabbing my wrist.

'Oh yes I do,' I screamed, trying to tug myself away.

'Will you stop behaving like a whore!' he swore at me and, pulling me into the nearest bedroom, threw me on the bed and locked the door.

'Now I suppose you're going to treat me like a whore,' I spat at him. 'What will your precious Lorna say if she catches us here together?'

Suddenly I was frightened. There was murder in his eyes.

'It's about time someone taught you a lesson,' he said,

coming towards me. 'And I'm afraid it's going to be me.'

Before I realized it, Gareth had me across his knee. I've never known what living daylights were before, but he was certainly beating them out of me now. I started to scream and kick.

'Shut up,' he said viciously. 'No one can hear you.' The record player was still booming downstairs. I struggled and tried to bite him but he was far too strong for me. It was not the pain so much as the ghastly indignity. It seemed to go on for ever and ever. Finally he tipped me on to the floor. I lay there trembling with fear.

'Get up,' he said brusquely, 'and get your things together. I'm taking you back to the boat.'

The moon hung over the river, whitening the mist that floated transparent above the sleeping fields. Stars were crowding the blue-black sky, the air was heavy with the scent of meadow-sweet.

Aching in every bone, biting my lip to stop myself crying, I let Gareth lead me across the fields. Every few moments I stumbled, held up only by his vice-like grip on my arm. I think he felt at any moment I might bolt back to the party.

Once we were on deck I said, 'Now you can go back to your darling teenager.'

'Not until you're safe in bed.'

I lay down on my bunk still in my dress. But when I shut my eyes the world was going round and round. I quickly opened them. Gareth stood watching me through cigar smoke.

I shut my eyes again. A great wave of nausea rolled over me.

'Oh God,' I said, trying to get out of bed.

'Stay where you are,' he snapped.

'I ought to be allowed to get out of my own bed,' I said petulantly. 'I agree in your Mary Whitehouse role you're quite entitled to stop me getting into other people's beds but a person should be free to get out of her own bed if she wants to.'

'Stop fooling around,' said Gareth.

'I can't,' I said in desperation, 'I'm going to be sick.'

He only just got me to the edge of the boat in time, and I was sicker than I've ever been in my life. I couldn't stop this terrible retching, and then, because Gareth was holding my head, I couldn't stop crying from humiliation.

'Leave me alone,' I sobbed in misery. 'Leave me alone to die. Gussie and Jeremy'll be back in a minute. Please go and keep them away for a bit longer.'

'They won't be back for hours,' said Gareth, looking at his watch.

'Can I have a drink of water?'

'Not yet, it'll only make you throw up again. You'll just have to grin and bear it.'

I looked up at the huge white moon and gave a hollow laugh. 'It couldn't be a more romantic night, could it?'

In the passage my knees gave way and Gareth picked me up, carried me into the cabin and put me to bed as deftly as if I'd been a child. He gave me a couple of pills.

'They'll put you to sleep.'

'I wasn't actually planning to meet Jeremy on deck tonight.'

I was shivering like a puppy.

'I'm sorry,' I said, rolling my head back and forth on the pillow. 'I'm so terribly sorry.'

'Lie still,' he said. 'The pills'll work soon.'

'Don't go,' I whispered, as he stood up and went to the door.

His face was expressionless as he looked at me, no scorn, no mockery, not even a trace of pity.

'I'm going to get you some more blankets,' he said. 'I don't want you catching cold.'

That sudden kindness, the first he'd ever shown me, brought tears to my eyes. I was beginning to feel drowsy by the time he came back with two rugs. They smelt musty and, as I watched his hands tucking them in—powerful hands with black hairs on the back—I suddenly wanted to feel his arms around me and to feel those hands soothing me and petting me as though I were a child again. In a flash I saw him as the father, strict, yet loving and caring, that all my life I'd missed; someone to say stop when I went too far, someone to mind if I behaved badly, to be proud if I behaved well.

'Getting sleepy?' he asked.

I nodded.

'Good girl. You'll be all right in the morning.'

'I'm sorry I wrecked your party.'

'Doesn't matter. They're nice though, the Hamiltons. You should mix with more people like them; they've got the right values.'

'How did you meet them?'

He began to tell me, but I started getting confused and the soft Welsh voice became mingled with the water lapping against the boat; then I drifted into unconsciousness.

12

When I woke next morning I felt overwhelmed with shame. In the past when I'd got drunk, I'd just shrugged it off as part of the Octavia Brennen image. Now I curled up at the thought of last night's performance—barging in on those people half naked, behaving atrociously, abusing their hospitality, and then the humiliation of Gareth putting me across his knee and, worst of all, throwing up in front of him and having to be put to bed.

Oh God, I groaned in misery, as I slowly pieced the evening together, I can't face him. Yet, at the thought of slipping off the boat unnoticed, it suddenly hit me that if I did I might never see him again. It was like a skewer jabbed into my heart.

Oh no, I whispered in horror, it can't have happened! I couldn't hate someone so passionately, and then find overnight that hatred had turned into something quite different—something that looked suspiciously like love.

I couldn't love him, I couldn't. He despised me and thought I was the biggest bitch going, and the nightmare was that, if we had been starting from scratch, I could have pulled out the stops, knocked him over with my looks, even fooled him into thinking I was gentle and sweet. I'd done it often enough before. But now it was too late. He'd seen me, unashamedly pursuing Jeremy, knew so many adverse things about me that I hadn't a hope where he was concerned. It was funny really, the biter bit at last.

Finally I dragged myself out of bed. A shooting star was erupting in my head, waves of sickness swept over me. My face was ashen when I looked in the mirror. I was still wearing last night's make-up, streaked with crying; my mouth felt like a parrot's cage.

I staggered down to the horrible dank loo which reeked of asparagus pee and wondered whether to be sick again. Even cleaning my teeth was an ordeal. Somehow I got dressed, and crawled along to the kitchen. Gussie was cooking kippers of all things.

'Hullo,' she said. 'You disappeared very suddenly last night. Gareth said you felt faint from the heat, so he brought you home. You're not pregnant or anything awful?'

I smiled weakly and shook my head. That was one problem I was spared.

'What did the rest of you get up to?' I asked.

'Nothing much. We stayed up very late dancing on the lawn, it was so romantic in the moonlight. Then Lorna came back and had a drink on the boat. You were fast asleep by that time. Later Gareth took her home. We didn't hear him come in.'

I felt sweat rising on my forehead. The thought of Gareth and Lorna wandering back through the meadowsweet with that great moon pouring light on them drove me insane with jealousy. The smell of those kippers was killing me. Suddenly I saw a pair of long legs coming down the steps.

'I'm going on deck,' I said in a panic, and bolted back through my cabin and the saloon, out into the sunshine at the far end of the boat.

I sat down, clutching my knees and gazing at the opposite bank. A water rat came out, stared at me with beady eyes and then shot back into its hole. Lucky thing, I thought. I wish I had a hole to crawl into. The wild roses which had bloomed so beautifully yesterday were now withered by the sun and hung like tawdry party decorations that had been up too long.

I heard a step behind me and my heart started hammering. I was appalled by the savagery of my disappointment when I realized it was only Jeremy.

'Hullo,' he said sulkily, sitting down beside me. 'Are you feeling better?'

'Yes thank you.'

'Gareth gets all the luck. Why don't you feel faint when I'm around? I wouldn't have minded bringing you back here on your own and putting you to bed.'

Something in his voice pulled me up sharply. 'I felt faint,' I snapped.

'And I'm sure Gareth made you feel better. His restorative powers are notorious, you know.'

'It wasn't like that,' I said angrily. 'If two people absolutely don't fancy each other, it's Gareth and me.'

'So you keep telling me,' he said. 'I'm wondering if the lady isn't protesting a bit too much.'

'Breakfast's ready,' said Gareth, appearing suddenly in the doorway.

'I don't want any,' I said, blushing scarlet and wondering how much of our conversation he'd heard.

Jeremy got to his feet.

'I'll come back and talk to you when I've had mine,' he said, following Gareth down the steps.

Two minutes later Gareth reappeared.

'Here's your breakfast,' he said, dropping four Alka Seltzers into a glass of water. He waited until the white discs had completely dissolved, then handed me the glass.

'Thank you,' I muttered, quite unable to meet his eyes. 'I'm sorry about last night.'

'Skip it,' he said. 'Everyone makes a bloody fool of themselves from time to time.'

'But you stopped everyone else finding out. I thought . . .'

'. . . I'd go back and tell everyone you'd puked your guts out. I'm not that much of a sod.'

I looked at him for the first time. He looked very tired; there were dark rings under his eyes. I wondered what he and Lorna had been up to last night. It was as though he'd read my thought.

'Lorna's coming over for lunch,' he said. 'She's dying to meet you again. She's still at the age when she's immensely impressed by beautiful women.'

Wow, that was a backhander.

'I'll attempt not to disappoint her,' I said, trying to keep the resentment out of my voice.

He laughed. 'Don't pout, it doesn't suit you.'

The Alka Seltzers eased my headache to a dull throb. I wished it could have as easily cured my heart.

Lorna arrived about twelve-thirty. She'd taken a great deal of trouble with her appearance and was wearing a rust coloured T-shirt which matched her hair. She looked very pretty, but somehow I thought she'd looked more attractive when she'd roared in on us unawares the day before.

'Hullo,' she said, sitting down on the deck beside me, 'I'm sorry we didn't have time to talk yesterday and that you felt horrible. Mummy always forgets to open any windows. Everyone was so disappointed you went. All the men were wild about you, and everyone who rang up to thank us this morning wanted to know who you were.' Her voice was suddenly wistful. 'The country hasn't seen anything as gorgeous as you in a hundred years.'

Suddenly I found myself liking her. I realized there was no bitchy motive behind her remarks, just genuine admiration.

'I'm afraid my dress was a bit *outré* for the country,' I said. 'I hope your parents didn't mind?'

She shook her head violently. 'Oh no, they thought you were wonderful. It's typical of Gareth to turn up with someone like you. I always knew he would in the end. I've had a crush on him for years, you see. I'd always hoped he'd wait for me, but now he's got you.'

'Oh no he hasn't,' I said quickly. 'There's nothing between us at all. We'd never met before this weekend. I'm Gussie's friend. We were at school together.'

'You were?' Her face brightened. 'Then you and Gareth aren't . . .?'

'Not at all. He just discovered I was feeling bloody and brought me home.'

'Oh,' she said happily. 'That does cheer me up. I do wish I could do something romantic like fainting when he's around, but I'm far too healthy.'

I laughed wryly. She wouldn't have enjoyed what I'd endured last night.

'Mind you,' she went on confidingly, 'he did kiss me on the way home last night. But then I expect he kisses most girls.'

The sun was making me feel sick again. I moved into the shade. She asked me endless questions about my life in London and the people I knew.

'Do you actually know Mick Jagger?' She couldn't hear enough about it.

'I'm coming to London soon. I've just finished a typing course, and I've got to look for a job.'

'Come and stay,' I was amazed to find myself saying. 'My flat's huge. You can have a bed for as long as you like.'

'Goodness,' she went all pink. 'May I really? It'd be marvellous, just for a few days until I find somewhere. And I wonder, could you tell me the best place to buy clothes? I mean my mother's super, but she's never been much help in that way.'

A moment later, when we were joined by the others, she immediately told Gareth I'd asked her to come and stay. I expected him to discourage her, but he merely said, 'Good idea, why not?'

Why had I done it, I wondered, as I escaped to help with lunch. Was I trying to prove that I could be nice occasionally, or was I unconsciously trying to impress Gareth by getting on with one of his friends, or was it merely that I wanted to keep some link with him, however tenuous, after tonight?

I had a great deal of difficulty forcing anything down at lunch. I couldn't even smoke, which is a sign of approaching death with me. I was paralysed with shyness by Gareth's presence. Every time he looked at me I jerked my eyes away. Why couldn't I bring any of the old magic into play? Glancing sideways from under my lashes, letting my hair fall over my eyes, pulling up my skirt to show more leg, leaning forward so he could see down my shirt, which would always be buttoned a couple of inches too low. Overnight I'd suddenly become as gauche as a teenager. I didn't even know what to do with my mouth—like the first time one wears lipstick.

To make matters worse, Jeremy was watching me like a warder. He no longer held any charm for me; he was so anxious to please, he'd lost all the lazy, take-it-or-leave-it manner that I'd found so irresistible a week ago. Immediately we'd finished eating, I leapt up to do the washing up. Anything to get away from that highly charged atmosphere.

'Leave it,' said Jeremy. 'For goodness sake, Octavia, relax.'

'What a bore we're going back to London tonight,' grumbled Gussie. 'It's been such a lovely restful weekend.'

A smile flickered across Gareth's face.

'You must have so much planning to do for the wedding,' Lorna said. 'I love weddings.'

Jeremy's leg suddenly pressed against mine. I moved it away.

'Your hair's gone a fantastic colour in the sun,' he said.

'Is it natural, I can't remember?' said Gussie.

I was about to say 'yes'—I'd never admitted to anyone before that it was dyed—when I caught Gareth's eye and, for some strange reason, changed my mind.

'Well, let's say my hairdresser helps it along a bit.'

Gussie picked up a daisy chain she'd been making. The threaded flowers were already wilting on the table. Lorna looked out of the port-hole at the heat-soaked landscape. Any moment one felt the dark trees might move towards us.

'It's like one of those days people remember as the end of something,' she said, 'The last before the war, the day the king died.'

Gussie split another daisy stalk open. 'Don't frighten me, you make me think something frightful will happen tonight.'

A mulberry-coloured cloud had hidden the sun.

'I think it's going to thunder,' said Jeremy.

Gussie put the daisy chain over his head. It was too small and rested like a coronet on his blond hair. He pushed it away irritably.

'Oh, you've broken it,' wailed Gussie.

I couldn't stand the tension any longer. I got to my feet and stretched.

'Where are you off to?' said Gussie.

'I'm going to wander up-stream.'

'We'll come with you,' said Jeremy standing up.

'No!' I said sharply, then tried to make a joke of it. 'I like walking by myself. I feel my Greta Garbo mood coming on.'

'We're going to Lorna's parents for tea,' said Gussie.

I didn't join them. As I wandered through the meadows I tried to sort out what I really felt. It's the heat and the proximity I kept telling myself. You've fallen for Gareth because he's the first man to pull you up. It's a challenge because he doesn't fancy you—just as Jeremy was a challenge until you'd hooked him. But it was no good. Wanting Jeremy had been but a child's caprice for a forbidden toy, nothing compared with the desperate need I felt for Gareth.

I wandered for miles and then sat down under a tree. I must have dozed off, for the shadows were lengthening when I woke up. I couldn't face tea with the Hamiltons, teacups balanced on our knees, having post mortems about the party; so I went back to the boat. No one was about. I packed my suitcases, tidied the saloon and washed up lunch. I was behaving so well, I'd be qualifying for my girl guide badge at this rate.

Then I heard footsteps, and someone jumping on to the deck. I gave a shiver of excitement as a tall figure appeared in the doorway. But it was only Jeremy. Once more I felt that crippling kick of disappointment.

'Why didn't you turn up for tea? I've been worried about you.'

There was a predatory look in his eyes that suddenly had me scared and on my guard.

'I fell asleep and when I woke up I realized it was late, so I came back here.'

'And by telepathy I knew and followed you,' he said.

'Are the others coming?'

'Not for ages. Gussie's discovered a grand piano, so she's happy strumming away. Gareth and Lorna have gone off for a walk together.'

My nails were cutting into the palms of my hands. Last night Gareth had kissed her. God knows what else he might get up to on a hot summer afternoon. I picked up some glasses.

'Where are you going?' asked Jeremy.

'Putting these away.'

For a second he barred my way, then stood aside and followed me through into the saloon. Very slowly I stacked the glasses in the cupboard. When I turned round he was standing just behind me. He put his hands on my arms.

'No,' I said sharply.

'No what? I haven't done anything yet.'

'Then let me go.'

'The hell I will!'

His fingers tightened on my arms.

'I want you,' he said. 'Ever since I first saw you, I've been burning up with wanting you.'

'What about Gussie?' I asked feebly. 'We were going to wait till we got back to London.'

'Oh come *on* now. You, of *all* people, don't give a damn about Gussie, and at this moment in time, neither do I.'

He bent his head and kissed me, forcing my mouth open with his tongue.

'No!' I struggled, completely revolted. 'No! No! No!'

'Shut up,' he said. 'Don't play the little hypocrite with me.

We all know your reputation, darling. You wanted me, don't pretend you didn't, and now you're going to get me, hot and strong.'

Desperately, I tried to pull away from him.

'Let me go!' I screamed.

But he only laughed and forced me back on to one of the bench seats, shutting my protesting mouth with his, tearing at the buttons of my shirt.

Suddenly a door opened. 'Knock it off you two,' said a voice of ice.

Jeremy sprang away from me. 'What the fuck . . .'

'For God's sake pull yourself together. Gussie's just coming,' said Gareth.

But it was too late, Gussie came bouncing into the saloon.

'Darling love, I missed you. Hullo Tavy, did you get lost?'

Then, with agonizing slowness, she took in the situation, looking at my rumpled hair and torn shirt, the buttons of which I was frenziedly trying to do up, the smeared lipstick on Jeremy's face, the chair knocked over, the papers strewn all over the floor.

There was a ghastly pause.

'Octavia,' she whispered in horror. 'You of all people, how could you? You swore you weren't interested in Jeremy. I thought you were a friend of mine. And as for you!' She turned to Jeremy, 'Don't you think I want to marry you after this.'

She tugged at her engagement ring but it wouldn't come off. Finally she gave a little sob and fled out of the cabin.

'Go after her!' said Gareth. 'Say you're sorry, that it didn't mean anything—at once,' he rapped out at Jeremy.

I collapsed into a chair, my heart pounding, my face in my hands. 'Oh my God, how terrible!'

'And you can belt up,' Gareth snarled at me. 'You've done enough damage for one afternoon.'

'I tried to stop him, really I did.'

'Don't give me that. There's no need to explain yourself. You were just running true to form.' And he walked out of the saloon, slamming the door behind him.

The awful thing was that we still had to pack up the boat and Lorna had to drive us to the original mooring twenty miles away, where Jeremy and Gareth had parked their cars. Gussie insisted on sitting in the back with Gareth and sobbing all the way. Jeremy and I, loathing each other's guts, had to sit in front with Lorna.

When we finally got to where the cars were parked, Gussie refused to drive back to London with Jeremy. Gareth didn't even say goodbye.

God, how ironic, I thought miserably, it's worked out exactly as I planned it should. Gussie and Jeremy breaking up and Jeremy driving me back to London. But instead of being in each other's arms, we were at each other's throats. Jeremy looked grey beneath his suntan, all the bravado and panache seemed to be knocked out of him. The trees by the roadside fell away and rushed back in clumps.

'You've got to talk to Gussie,' said Jeremy. 'Tell her it was all your fault. All right, I admit I tried to pull you this afternoon, but my God, I had provocation.'

'I know you did,' I said listlessly. 'I'm sorry. I thought I wanted you so much; then when it came to the crunch, I found I didn't after all.'

'Yeah well, it's the same with me. I was crazy about you, but now I realize I'm in danger of losing Gus, it all seems a terrible mistake. It's the ill-wind department, I suppose. Takes a jolt like this to make you realize how much you really need someone. She's so straight, Gus.'

I'd seldom seen a man more shattered.

'Tell her it was your doing,' he pleaded. 'Tell her how much you led me on. It's no skin off your nose.'

'All right,' I said, 'I'll talk to her. But it's no good trying to see her until tomorrow.'

13

On the day after we got back to London, I tried to ring Gussie several times at the office. Finally they admitted she hadn't come in, so I went round to her flat. It was a typical girl's flat—unwashed cups and overflowing ashtrays everywhere and three half-unpacked suitcases in the drawing-room. I removed a grubby white bra and a brown apple core from one of the armchairs and sat down.

'What do you want?' asked Gussie. She was still in her dressing gown and her face was swollen with crying.

'To explain about Jeremy,' I said.

'I don't want any of your lies,' she said.

'But you've got to listen. It was all my fault, you see, from the beginning. I took one look at Jeremy that first night at Arabella's and he was so beautiful I decided I must get him away from you at all costs. I never wanted anyone so much in all my life so I pulled out all the stops—making eyes at him, admitting to his face that I fancied him, wandering round with only a towel falling off me, arranging to meet him on deck after you'd gone to sleep. He didn't stand a chance.'

She looked at me in horror. 'You actually went out of your way to get him?'

I nodded. 'I made an absolutely dead set that evening at the Hamilton's party,' I went on, lying now. 'When I got drunk and behaved so badly, it was only because I was furious with Jeremy, because he wasn't reacting at all.'

'But what happened yesterday?'

'I was sulking by myself on the boat, when Jeremy turned up, worried I'd been gone for such a long time, and well, I sort of tried to seduce him.'

'And that's when Gareth and I came in?'

'That's right.' I got up and wandered over to the window.

'Any man would have been flattered by being pursued so relentlessly. It was just the heat and being cooped up on the boat together. Hell, he only kissed me, anyway. He loves you, he does really. He was absolutely demented on the way home last night.'

Gussie pulled at a wispy bit of hair.

'He was?' she said dully.

'Anyway,' I went on, 'you said the other day on the boat, that you expected him to be unfaithful to you and you'd always forgive him.'

'I know I did,' said Gussie with a sob, 'but one says such stupid things in theory, and they're so horrible when they happen in practice.'

I went over and put my arm round her. 'Please don't cry, Gussie.'

'Don't touch me,' she hissed. 'I was thinking about you all last night. You're wicked, you've always been wicked. Ever since we were at school together, you've resented my friends and tried to take them away from me. And now you've stolen the most precious thing I ever had. Why do you do it? You're so beautiful you can have any man you choose.'

'Because I've always been jealous of you,' I said slowly, echoing Gareth's words. 'Because, in spite of my yellow hair and my long legs, people have always liked you more than they liked me.'

There was a pause.

'I suppose it was kind of you to come and tell me all this,' she said in a set little voice. 'It does make a difference. I had a long talk to Gareth last night.'

'What did he say?' I tried to keep my voice expressionless.

'That Jeremy was basically a lightweight, that I'd do better to cut my losses and pack him in. He said you may have encouraged Jeremy in the beginning, but on reflection he guessed that he was only too ready to be distracted and that it was Jeremy who forced the pace yesterday. He said marriage to Jeremy would be one long string of infidelities, and he was only marrying me for security and for my money.'

117

'But that's brutal!' I gasped.

'Isn't it? But that's the thing I like about Gareth, he tells the truth about things that matter.'

'Did he say anything else?' I said numbly. 'About me, I mean.'

'Not much. He agreed with me that if you really set your cap at someone, it would be almost impossible to resist you.'

I bit my lip. 'I'm sorry.'

'It's not so easy for me,' Gussie said, playing with the tassel of her dressing gown. 'I don't get boyfriends very easily. Jeremy was the first man who ever said he loved me. I can't go to a party tomorrow like you can, and pick up a new man just like that. I can't walk down the street and be caressed and comforted by the admiration in men's eyes. You haven't a clue what it's like not having any sex appeal. With you it's only a question of time. I may never meet another man who wants to marry me.'

I felt a flash of irritation. Why the hell didn't she go on a diet? Then I felt guilty.

'Will you ever be able to forgive me?'

'I don't know, not now. Perhaps in a few weeks I shall feel differently.'

I went towards the door.

'Will you see Jeremy if he turns up here?'

She burst into tears. 'Oh yes, of course I will.'

It was only when I left her that the full desolation of my situation hit me. Since we'd left the boat I had been numb with misery, as though I'd put my heart in deep freeze until I had straightened the account with Gussie and Jeremy. Now I had to face up to the future—to the agony of loving a man who hated and despised me—who would despise me even more once he heard what I had told Gussie.

For the next few days I was on the rack. I never believed it was possible to suffer so much. Pride, despair and longing chased each other monotonously around my head. I cried all night and, at the slightest provocation, during the day. Over and over again I wandered down to the river and wondered

whether to jump in. A thousand times I started letters to
Gareth, pleading my case, but each time I tore them up. My
case was so hopeless, I couldn't even take refuge in daydreams.

Most evenings I borrowed my landlord's car, drove it across
London and lay in wait outside Gareth's house, but there were
never any lights on and I used to turn the engine off and cry
uncontrollably.

14

The blistering hot weather continued to grip London by the
throat. Outside my flat Green Park was fast losing its green-
ness, the plane trees were coated in thick grey dust, the grass
bleached to a lifeless yellow. Commuters wilted silently at the
bus stops.

Two Mondays after we got back from the boat, I was woken
by the doorbell ringing on and on. Wrapping a towel round
me, I waded through the post, which was scattered over the
carpet and consisted entirely of brown envelopes. I peered
through the spy-hole, in a blind hope it might be Gareth. But it
was only a thin youth with a moustache, and ears like the F.A.
cup, wearing a crumpled suit and a battery of fountain pens in
his breast pocket. He obviously had no intention of getting off
that bell. I opened the door. He looked at me wearily.

'Miss Brennen?'

'No,' I said. I knew the tricks of old.

'But Miss Brennen lives here?'

'Sure she does, but she's abroad at the moment. Can I help
you?'

'It's about her income tax returns. We've written to her

repeatedly. The matter is getting rather urgent.'

'Oh dear,' I said sympathetically. 'I'm sure she's not avoiding you deliberately. She's just rather vague where income tax is concerned.'

'Lots of people become very vague when it's a matter of paying it,' he said, his weary eyes travelling over my body, 'When are you expecting her back?'

'She's gone to the Bahamas,' I said. 'After that I think she's flying on to New York. She's got a lot of friends there. She didn't say when she was coming back.'

'We're interested in a sum of money she earned doing a commercial for Herbert Revson.'

Thank God he was looking at my legs, or he would have seen how green I'd gone.

'But that was three years ago,' I stammered, 'and in America.'

'Yes, but she was paid by their English subsidiary, who, of course, declared it.'

'Poor Octavia,' I said faintly. 'Have you any idea how much she owes?'

'Well,' he said, confidingly. 'We don't usually disclose figures' (he was obviously crazy for me to disclose mine) 'but I think it wouldn't be much under five figures. She didn't by any chance leave a forwarding address, did she?'

'No she didn't. There's the telephone. I must go and answer it,' I said firmly, shutting the door in his face.

Ten thousand pounds! Where the hell was I going to get that kind of money? Bleating with terror, I ran to answer the telephone, crossing my fingers once again that by some miracle it might be Gareth. But it was Xander. I'd only talked to him briefly since I got back. He'd been busy, so I hadn't told him about Gareth. I was sure I wanted to, I couldn't bear for him not to take it seriously.

'Oh how lovely to hear you,' I said.

'You probably won't think so when you hear the news,' he said. 'Hugh Massingham's dead.'

'What!' I sat down on the bed.

'Heart attack at the weekend. He'd been playing tennis,' said Xander.

'Oh God, how awful.' Kind, handsome, indolent, sensual, easy-going Massingham—Xander's patron and boss, my friend. He's always been so generous to both of us—and taken care of all my bills. It didn't seem possible.

'I can't bear it,' I whispered, the tears beginning to roll down my cheeks.

'Terrible, isn't it. I really loved that guy. But darling, I'm afraid that isn't all. There's trouble at mill. Ricky's been going through the books with a toothcomb and smelling salts, and the skeletons have been absolutely trooping out of the cupboard. This year's figures are catastrophic, shares have hit rock bottom, orders are right down; unfortunately expenses, particularly yours, and mine, are right up.'

He sounded in a real panic.

'Ricky's called an emergency department head meeting for tomorrow at three o'clock. He wants you there as well.'

'Whatever for?'

'Well, there's a bit of aggro over your flat, and all the bills we've run up between us, and there's the car too. I think we'd better have a session tonight, and see how many bills we can rustle up,' he went on, trying to sound reassuring.

'All right,' I said. 'Come round after work.'

It seemed hardly the time to tell him about my income tax bill.

'Actually,' Xander went on, 'it's a good thing poor Hugh did kick the bucket when he did, Ricky'd already made plans to replace him.'

'Did Hugh know?'

'Don't think so, but it's certainly made Ricky's task easier. He's bringing in this new whizz kid over everyone's heads to get us out of the wood.'

'Do you think he'll be able to?'

'You should know, darling. It's your friend, Gareth Llewellyn.'

I lay back on my bed, holding my burning face in my hands

—all thoughts of Massingham, ten grand tax bills and fiddled expenses forgotten. Why, why, why had Gareth done it? He'd got far too much on his plate as it was. Why should he take on another directorship? Was it for power, or financial gain, or just to get his fingers into another industrial pie? Could it just possibly be that he wanted to see me again? Or, much more likely, that he'd got it in for me and wanted to cut me to ribbons. Whatever the reason, in just over twenty-four hours I'd see him again.

In the evening Xander and I spent two fruitless hours trying to sort out our expenses—then gave up. I set my alarm clock for eleven the next day, to give me plenty of time to get ready. Even so I panicked round trying on one dress after another. It's strange how one's wardrobe tells the story of one's past. There was the cornflower blue midi I'd bought to ensnare Jeremy, the backless black that had inflamed Ricardo, the gold pyjama suit that had brought Charlie literally to his knees with a proposal, and lying on the cupboard floor, spurned, and never worn again, was the grey dress that had failed to detach that French racing driver from his wife at a ball in Paris last winter.

What could I possibly wear to win over Gareth? He'd said he liked his women gentle, unspoilt and vulnerable. I put on a white dress, bought for Ascot last year, but never worn. It was very garden party, with a full skirt, long sleeves and a ruffled low-cut neckline which showed off my suntan and I hoped made me look innocent and fragile. I had to make a hole in the material to do the belt up tight enough. My eyelids, after a fortnight's crying, were the only part of me that hadn't lost weight. I hid them behind tinted spectacles.

I arrived at Seaford-Brennen's head office to find everyone in a jittering state of expectancy. Yesterday's shock over Massingham's death had given way to excitement over Gareth's arrival. The secretaries had seen his picture on the financial pages. They knew he was rich, successful, attractive and, most important of all, single. They had all washed their hair and tarted themselves up to the nines. The offices, as I walked through, smelt like Harrods' scent department; not a paper was out of place. I encountered some hostile stares. Why did I have to come swanning in to steal their thunder?

The Seaford-Brennen boardroom, with its dove grey carpet, panelled walls and family portraits, was discretion itself. Xander was the only person in there, sitting halfway down the huge polished table, directly beneath the portrait of my father. Their two bored, handsome restless faces were so much alike. Xander was chewing gum, and drawing a rugger player on his pad.

'Hullo angel,' he said in a slurred voice as I slipped into the seat beside him. 'The condemned board is still out eating a hearty lunch. This place is in an incredible state of twitch, even the messenger boys are on tranquillizers. Ricky's already been on to me this morning breathing fire about expenses. You must keep bills. I said I'm already keeping a Pamela, what would I want with a Bill.'

Oh God, I thought, he's smashed out of his mind; he must be chewing gum to conceal the whisky fumes.

'What happened after you left me?' I said.

'I went out and dined, not wisely, but too well, with a friend, and things escalated from there.'

'Did you get to bed?'

'Well not to my own bed, certainly.' He tried to rest an elbow on the table, but it slid off.

The door opened and Miss Billings, the senior secretary, came in, fussing around, moving memo pads, straightening pencils. A great waft of Devon violets nearly asphyxiated us.

'You ought to put a bit more Pledge at the top of the table,' said Xander reprovingly, 'and I'm rather surprised you haven't laid on a red carpet and a band playing "Land of my Fathers". Mr. Llewellyn is used to the best of everything you know.'

Miss Billings clicked her tongue disapprovingly and bustled out, beads flying. Next moment she was back, with Tommy Lloyd, the sales director.

'Do you think we ought to put flowers in the middle of the table?' she asked.

'A bunch of leeks would be more appropriate,' said Xander.

Tommy Lloyd gave him a thin smile. He tolerated Xander but didn't like him. An old Wellingtonian with a bristling grey moustache, ramrod straight back, and clipped military voice, he had been in next succession after Massingham. His red-veined nose must be truly out of joint at Gareth's arrival. He was followed by Peter Hocking, who was in charge of production and just about as inspiring as a flat bottle of tonic, and old Harry Somerville, his false teeth rattling with nerves, who'd been with the firm since he was sixteen, and was still treated by everyone as though he was a messenger boy.

Gradually the rest of the chairs were taken up by departmental heads, flushed by lunch, who greeted me with a good deal less enthusiasm than usual, a far cry from the fawning sycophancy when my father was alive.

There was desultory talk of our chances of winning the Test match. Peter Hocking was boring Harry Somerville with a recipe for home-made wine. But on the whole everyone was strangely quiet, and kept glancing at their watches or the door.

'When all else fails, go to Wales,' said Xander. 'I feel exactly as though I'm about to go over Niagara Falls in a barrel. Have you got a cigarette? I seem to have run out.'

I gave him one and, having opened my bag, took the opportunity to powder my nose and put on some more scent. My hand was shaking so much, I put on far too much. The smell of Miss Dior wafting through the room, clashed vilely with the Devon violets.

'Never mind,' said Xander. 'At least it will cover up the smell of congealed blood and rotting corpses.'

He seemed strangely elated. He'd always liked novelty. There were little red patches along his cheekbones.

The waiting got worse. Everyone's shirt collars were getting too tight. Miss Billings sat on the right of the top of the table, flicking the elastic band which held back the pages on which she had already taken shorthand that day. We all jumped when the telephone rang.

Tommy Lloyd answered.

'Downstairs are they? Good. Well no doubt Ricky'll bring them up. Miss Billings, will you go and meet them at the lift.'

'The enemy are at the gates,' said Xander, still drawing rugger players on his memo pad. 'The Barbarian Hoards are coming. I suppose we'd better lie back and enjoy it.'

There was a spurt of nervous laughter round the room, which died quickly away as the door opened. They came in like the magnificent four, Ricky smirking as though he was carrying a very large bone, followed by Gareth, and a huge, massive-shouldered wrestler of a man in a white suit. Bringing up the rear was Annabel Smith. She was wearing a very simple black suit, and her conker-coloured hair was drawn back in a chignon. The dead silence that followed was a tribute to her beauty. Suddenly I felt silly in my white dress, like a deb who'd been left out in the rain.

I was so wraked with longing and shyness, it was a second before I could bring myself to look at Gareth. He was wearing a light grey suit, dark blue shirt and tie. I'd never seen him so formally dressed. His heavy face had lost most of its suntan, and looked shadowed and tired. He didn't glance in my direction.

Everyone sat down except Ricky, who stood for a minute looking silently round the table, as if counting the house.

'Shall I bring in coffee now?' said Miss Billings fussily.

'I don't think we need it, thank you,' he said. 'And you needn't bother to stay either, Miss Billings. Mrs. Smith is going to take the minutes.'

Displaying the same sort of enraged reluctance as a cat shoved out in a rainstorm, Miss Billings was despatched from the room. Any minute I expected her to appear at the window, mewing furiously.

Ricky cleared his throat.

'Gentlemen, I just want to introduce Mr. Llewellyn whom I'm sure you all know by repute. He's brought with him his right hand man, Mr. Morgan,'—the massive wrestler nodded at us unsmilingly—'and his very charming personal assistant, Mrs. Smith, who together have been responsible for so much of Mr. Llewellyn's success.'

Mrs. Smith gave everyone the benefit of her pussy-cat smile. Round the table a few faces brightened. Mrs. Smith's legs were a much better reason for staying awake in meetings than Miss Billings'.

'Although Mr. Llewellyn has come in at very short notice,' Ricky went on, 'as your new', he paused on the word, 'overall director, he has, as you know, many other commitments, so we mustn't expect to monopolize too much of his time. He has, however, been examining the structure of Seaford-Brennen's for some weeks, and has come up with some very useful suggestions, but nothing for anyone to get alarmed about.'

'What about Hugh Massingham?' said Xander's slurred voice. Everyone looked round in horror, as though one of the portraits had spoken. There was an embarrassed pause. Xander went on carefully putting the stripes on a rugger shirt. I didn't dare look at Gareth.

'I was just coming to that,' said Ricky, with a slight edge in his voice. 'I know how upset you must be all over Hugh's death. As a close personal friend and a colleague for many years, I know how much I'm going to miss him, and how our sympathy goes out to his widow and family. I hope as many of you as possible will go to the memorial service on the 5th. In the meantime,' he said, going into top gear with relief, 'it was vital to restore public confidence immediately and prevent a further fall on the stock market, so we invited Mr. Llewellyn to join the board.'

To avoid any further interruption from Xander, he hastily started introducing Gareth round the table. Tommy Lloyd shook hands, but was obviously bristling with antagonism, nor did any of the other department heads look particularly friendly. Poor Gareth, he was obviously in for a rough ride. It seemed an eternity before they came to me. I was sure the whole room could hear my heart hammering.

'You know Octavia,' said Ricky.

Gareth's eyes were on me. They were hard and flinty, without trace of the former laughing gypsy wickedness.

126

'Yes, I know Octavia,' he said grimly.

The flinty glance moved on to Xander.

'And this is Octavia's brother, my son-in-law, Alexander,' said Ricky, as though he was daring Xander to speak out of turn.

Xander got to his feet. 'Heil Hitler,' he said with a polite smile, hiccoughed and sat down.

'Xander!' thundered Ricky.

'I know that in welcoming Mr. Llewellyn,' said old Harry Somerville, his Adam's apple bobbing furiously, 'I speak for everyone in saying how pleased we all are.'

'Balls,' said Xander.

'Xander,' snapped Ricky, 'if you can't keep a civil tongue in your head you'd better bugger off.'

All the same I had a chilling feeling that he was delighted Xander was playing up, so that Gareth could see what provocation he normally had to put up with.

'Well, I think it's over to you now, Gareth,' he added, sitting down.

Gareth got to his feet, still unsmiling, but completely relaxed. For a second he upended a memo pad on the table, swinging it reflectively between finger and thumb, then he looked round like a conductor waiting until he had everyone's attention.

'I'd like to kick off by examining the structure of the company,' he said. 'As Mr. Seaford has already indicated, I've been studying your outfit for a few weeks, and I've come to the conclusion—and I'm going to be brutal—that your whole organization needs to be restructured from top to bottom, and that some people, particularly those at the top, are going to have to pull their fingers out.'

He then proceeded to launch a blistering attack on Seaford-Brennen's managerial hierarchy, its distribution of assets, and its work in progress, which left everyone reeling. Tommy Lloyd was looking like an enraged beetroot, the rest of the table as though they were posing for a bad photograph. There was no doubt that Gareth could talk. He had all the Welsh gift of the gab, the eloquence, the magnetism, the soft cadences. You might hate what he said, but you had to listen.

'I called this meeting in the afternoon,' he went on, 'because with your track record, I didn't think you'd all manage to make it in the morning. Half of you seem to feel it's only worth putting in an hour's work before going to lunch. One can never get any of you before 10.30 or after 5.0, not to mention the three hours you all spend in the middle of the day, roughing it at the Ritz.'

Tommy Lloyd's lips tightened. 'While we rough it at the Ritz, as you so politely call it,' he said coldly, 'most of the company business is done.'

'Not on the evidence of the order books,' said Gareth. 'You've got to wake up to the fact that the old boy network is dead—all that palsy walsy back-scratching over triple Remy Martins doesn't count for anything any more, and you've got to stand on your own feet too. You've got too used to relying on government subsidies or massive loans from the parent company, and when they run out you squeal for more.' He looked round the table. 'When did any of you last go to the factory?' he said, suddenly changing tack.

There was an embarrassed shuffling silence.

'We're in frequent telephonic communication,' said Peter Hocking in his thick voice.

'That's not good enough,' said Gareth banging his hand down on the table so loudly that everyone jumped. 'I know, because I've been up to Glasgow, *and* Coventry *and* Bradford in the last few days and morale is frightful. No wonder you're crippled by strikes.'

'You should know, of course,' said Tommy Lloyd, thoroughly nettled. 'I was forgetting you're one of the new establishments without roots or responsibility.'

'Do you think I've got 50,000 employees,' Gareth snapped, 'without any kind of responsibility? Sure, I did my stint on the factory floor, so I happen to know men work, not just for a pay packet, but because they're proud of what they produce, and because the people they work for care about them. You lot think as long as you give the staff a gold watch after fifty years' hard grind, and a booze-up at Christmas, and then forget about them, it's enough. In my companies,' he went on, the Welsh accent becoming more pronounced, 'we tell everyone what's going on. We have a policy of employee participation. We even have someone from the shop floor in on board meetings. A blue print of the company's future is regularly circulated to all staff. It brings them in, makes them feel they belong. Every worker can ask the management a question and feel sure of getting an answer.'

He was stunning. There is nothing more seductive than seeing the person one loves excelling in a completely unexpected field. I wanted to throw bouquets and shout 'Bravo'.

Tommy Lloyd's lips, however, were curling scornfully.

'Good of you to give us your advice, Mr. Llewellyn,' he said. 'That kind of Utopian concept may work in the building industry, but I don't get the impression you know much about engineering. We've been running our own show very successfully, you know, for fifty years.'

'That's the trouble. Seaford-Brennen's was a first class family firm, but you've been living on your reputation for the last twenty years.'

'We've got the finest, most advanced research department in the country,' said Tommy Lloyd, stung, but still smiling.

'That's the trouble again,' said Gareth. 'Lots of research, and none of it applied. Two months ago I came back from a world trip. The Brush Group and British Electrical were everywhere, you were nowhere. I'm sorry, but it's the truth.'

Tommy Lloyd picked up a cigar and started paring off the end.

Gareth turned to Kenny Morgan who handed him a couple of sheets of paper.

'Kenny's been looking into your books,' said Gareth.

'He's no right to,' said Tommy Lloyd, turning purple.

'He calculates you won't even make a profit next year, certainly not £8 million as you forecast. That's a lot of bread.'

'I consider that a gross breach of security,' said Tommy

Lloyd, addressing Ricky directly.

Ricky ignored him and continued looking at Gareth, who went on softly:

'And if anything, Kenny's estimate is still too high. All I'm saying is you need help in running your business, and I intend to make it what it's never been—efficient. You've got to face up to international competition: Americans, Germans, Japs, Russians. Last year I saw some industrial complexes in Siberia running at a fraction of our costs. If we're going to beat the Russians at their own game, there's no room for companies with a purely domestic market.

'And your domestic figures aren't very pretty, either,' he added. 'You all know they've sagged from 15.2 per cent of the home market four years ago to 4 per cent today.'

He paused, stretching his fingers out on the table, and examining them for a minute.

'Now, what is the solution?' he said, looking round the table.

Xander drew the bar across a pair of rugger posts.

'I think we'd all better start practising the goose step,' he said.

There was an awful silence. All eyes turned once more on Xander, but this time more with irritation than embarrassment. A muscle was going in Gareth's cheek.

'When I need a funny man,' he said sharply, 'I'll hire Morecambe and Wise. Do you personally have the answer to the problem?'

Xander leaned back for a minute to admire his artwork.

'Well, not right here in my pocket,' he said, and hiccoughed gently.

'Well shut up then,' snapped Gareth.

He got out a packet of cigarettes. Several lighters were raised, but he used his own, inhaling deeply, then said briskly:

'To get you out of the wood, Ricky and I suggest the following measures. To start with Seaford International is going to write off their £15 million loan as a loss, and give you a further £10 million over the next four years for a new model programme, and for modernizing the factories. Secondly, the existing products need more stringent tests. Practically everything you've produced recently has been blighted by poor reliability. Thirdly I intend to re-jig the production operation. It's got to be speeded up. Waiting lists are so long, buyers have been forced to go elsewhere. I'd like to have the new engines rolling off the assembly by January at the latest. And you're not producing enough either, so instead of laying off men at Glasgow and Bradford, we're going to initiate a second shift system. There are enough men up there who need work. Then it's up to you to sell them. That's your baby, Tommy.'

Tommy Lloyd turned puce at the casual use of his Christian name.

'We've got to completely re-think the export market too,' Gareth went on. 'The appetite in the Middle East and in Africa for your sort of stuff, particularly power stations, should produce thumping big orders.'

'You talk as though we've been sitting round since the war doing F . . . all,' said Tommy Lloyd stiffly. 'Anyone can put up proposals.'

'Exactly,' said Gareth. 'So let's get the ball rolling early tomorrow. Over the next fortnight Kenny and I plan to have talks with all of you individually. I won't be here all the time, but Kenny's going to put in a four-day week for the moment. Kenny,' he added, turning and looking at his manager's battered lugubrious face, 'I can assure you, is much tougher than he looks.'

A tremor of sycophantic laughter went through the room.

Gareth stood for a minute, looking cool, almost indifferent, but his left hand was squeezing the back of a chair so hard I could see the whiteness of his knuckles.

'I'm looking forward to working with you,' he said softly, 'but I'd like to add that I find it impossible to breathe or conduct business in a taut, patched-up regime; so you're either for me, or against me.'

And except for Xander, who was gazing blankly into space, and Tommy Lloyd, who was still looking livid, everyone seemed to be eating out of his hand. For a minute he glared at them grimly, then suddenly he smiled for the first time, the harsh, heavy features suddenly illuminated. The contrast was extraordinary; you could feel the tension going out of the room, as though you'd loosened your fingers on the neck of a balloon.

'I'm sorry I've been so blunt, but these things had to be said. You're in a hell of a mess, but frankly, I wouldn't have taken you on if I didn't think you could get yourselves out of it.'

When he sat down there was even a murmur of approval.

Ricky rose to his feet, oozing satisfaction like an over-ripe plum.

'Thank you, Gareth. I'm sure you can count on 100 per cent support. Now gentlemen, I believe that will be all today.'

There was a shuffling of feet. Everyone started to file out looking shell-shocked.

'I'll leave you then,' said Ricky. 'Again, many congratulations. We'll talk later today.'

I was dying to tell Gareth how great he'd been. But Annabel Smith was already doing it, speaking in an undertone, smiling warmly into his eyes, the predatory, self-possessed bitch.

Oh please at least let him say goodbye to me, I prayed, as I started towards the door.

Gareth turned. 'I want a word with you, Alexander, and you, Octavia,' he said shortly.

'Oh dear,' sighed Xander, 'I was afraid you might. Are we going to get a thousand lines, or is birching the only answer?'

15

As the last person shut the door behind them, Xander very slowly counted Mrs. Smith, me and Gareth with a shaking finger. Then he looked down at the long polished table.

'If we could find a net,' he said confidingly, 'we could have a ping-pong four.'

I giggled. Gareth and Mrs. Smith didn't. Xander pinched another of my cigarettes and went over to the window. We could hear the clunk of his signet ring as his fingers drummed nervously on the radiator. Gareth looked worn-out. I realized now what a strain the meeting had been.

'I wonder what's happening in the Test match,' said Xander to Mrs. Smith. 'You don't like cricket? Perhaps you had to play it at school like I did? Terrible for breaking one's finger nails.'

'That's enough,' snapped Gareth. 'I want to talk about your expenses.'

Xander and I sat quite still, not looking at each other. The temperature dropped to well below zero. My stomach gave a rumble like not so distant thunder. I'd only drunk cups of coffee since yesterday.

Gareth took a bit of paper from Mrs. Smith. 'We'll start with you, Alexander. Your U.K. expenses for the last month alone were well over two grand,' he said.

Xander removed his chewing gum reflectively, and parked it underneath the table.

'Arabs are dreadfully expensive to amuse,' he said.

'What Arabs?' asked Gareth. 'Not a single order has come from the Middle East to justify expenses like this.'

'Well it's in the pipeline,' said Xander. 'These things take time, you know.'

'I don't,' said Gareth brusquely. 'In most of these cases,

initial meetings were never followed up, some of them never took place at all. Mrs. Smith has been doing a bit of detective work. You claim to have taken a certain Sheik Mujab to the Clermont three times, and to Tramps twice over the past two months, but he says he's never heard of you.'

'He's lying,' blustered Xander. 'They all do.'

'And Jean-Baptiste Giraud of Renault's,' Gareth ran his eyes down the page, 'appears to have had nearly £400 spent on him during the last four weeks, being wined and dined by you and Octavia.'

'Octavia's a great asset with customers,' said Xander.

'I can well believe that,' said Gareth, in a voice of such contempt I felt myself go scarlet with humiliation. 'Unfortunately for you, Jean-Baptiste happens to be an old Oxford mate of mine. It took one telephone call to ascertain he only met you once over lunch at the Neal Street where he paid, and he's never met Octavia at all.'

'He must have forgotten,' said Xander.

'Don't be fatuous,' said Gareth. 'I don't hold much brief for your sister, but she's not the sort of girl an old ram like Jean-Baptiste would be likely to forget.'

I bit my lip. Annabel Smith was loving every minute of it.

'And so it goes on,' said Gareth. 'God knows how much you've cheated the shareholders out of—old ladies who've gambled their last savings, married couples with children who've hardly got a penny to rub together, and all the time you two've been treating the company like a bran tub, helping yourself as you choose.'

Xander started to play an imaginary violin. Gareth lost his temper.

'Can't you be fucking serious about anything? Haven't you any idea what an invidious position you've put Ricky in? He can't give you the boot because you're his son-in-law, but at the moment you're about as much good to him as a used tea bag.'

He walked over to the window, squinting at the traffic below, his huge shoulders hunched, his broken nose silhouetted against the blue sky, black and silver badger's hair curling thickly over his collar. I suddenly felt absolutely hollow with lust.

We all waited. As he turned round his expression hardened.

'I don't suppose I've ever come across a more greedy couple,' he said, speaking with swift curious harshness. 'I guess Massingham let you get away with it. I gather he was quite a fan of Octavia's.'

'Don't you dare say a word against Hugh,' I hissed. 'He was worth a million of you.'

Xander slumped in his chair. Suddenly to my horror I saw the tears pouring down his face. I put my arm round his shoulders.

'It's all right darling,' I said.

Once again Gareth changed tack and, with one of those staggering *volte faces*, said very gently,

'You were fond of him. I know. I'm sorry.'

Xander pushed back his hair and blinked two or three times.

'He was my friend, faithful and just to me,' he said slowly. 'But Ricky says he was incompetent. And Ricky is an honourable man, so they are all honourable men. Oh Christ, I should have had breakfast,' he added in a choked voice, groping for a handkerchief.

'Can't you leave him alone?' I screamed, turning on Gareth. 'Can't you see he isn't in any state for one of your bawlings out?'

'I'm sorry,' said Xander. 'When people call me Alexander, I always know they're cross with me.'

Gareth opened the window and threw out his lighted cigarette, seriously endangering the passers-by in the street below. Then he slammed the window shut and said to Xander in a businesslike tone,

'As I see it we have two alternatives. We could send you to prison for what you've been doing, or we can cart you onto the Board, which'll give you more money and enable you to start paying back some of the bread you've borrowed from the firm. It'll also mean we can keep a closer watch on your activities. You're bloody lucky you've got a rich and loyal wife.'

'The son-in-law also rises,' sighed Xander. 'I don't think I can accept your offer.'

'Don't be wet,' said Gareth brutally. 'I want you in the office by nine o'clock tomorrow, so we can re-jig the export schedule. In the meantime you'd better take a taxi home and sleep it off.'

'All the way to Sussex?' said Xander.

'You've got plenty of mates who'll put you up for the afternoon. Now beat it.'

Xander walked very unsteadily towards the door, cannoning off the table, the wall and two chairs. At the doorway he paused, looking anxiously at me, clearly about to say something in my defence, but was baulked by Gareth saying again, 'Go on, get out.'

There was an agonizing pause after he had gone. My stomach gave another earth-shattering rumble. I could feel my early morning cup of coffee sourly churning round inside me. I licked my lips.

'Now,' said Gareth grimly, 'what about you?' And he looked me over in a way that made me feel very small and uncomfortable and miserable.

'Can I go too?' I said, getting to my feet.

'Sit *down*.'

I sat.

'Annabel, can I have those other figures?' he said.

Annabel Smith handed him a pink folder at the same time putting a new tape in the machine. God, she was enjoying this.

'You should go cock-fighting next time,' I said to her. 'You'd find that even more exciting.'

'At the moment,' said Gareth, glancing down at the figures, 'you're living in a flat that's paid for by the firm. I also gather that, when you moved in three years ago, the firm coughed up at least seven grand to have it re-decorated. Since then Seaford-Brennen has not only been paying your 'phone bills and rates, but also the gas and electricity. And recently

Massingham gave you the Porsche on the firm which is costing a fortune to be repaired at the garage. There's also £3,500 worth of unspecified loans to be accounted for.'

There was another dreadful pause. All you could hear was the hiss of the tape-recorder.

'It wasn't just *my* flat,' I protested. 'Directors and clients often stayed there.'

'And you, I suppose, provided the service.'

'I bloody did not,' I said furiously. 'What d'you think I am—a flaming call girl?'

I was shaking with anger. I could feel my whole body drenched with sweat. Annabel Smith gazed out of the window and re-crossed her beautiful legs.

'Does she have to be here?' I went on. 'I suppose it's customary to have a woman cop present if you're going to beat up the prisoner. And can't you turn that bloody tape-recorder off?'

I imagined them playing it back to each other in bed, drinking Charles Heidsieck and laughing themselves sick. Gareth leaned forward and switched it off. Then he said:

'Annabel baby, go and get us some coffee, and see that Xander's safely put into a taxi.'

She smiled and left us, quietly closing the door behind her. I noticed with loathing that there wasn't a single crease in her black suit.

For a minute Gareth's fingers drummed on the table. Then he said,

'For the last three years you've been conducting your jet set existence entirely on the firm. Even if we write off your joint junketings with Xander, you owe nearly £6,000. I want you out of that flat by the end of the month and I want the keys to your company car tomorrow. Here are your last quarter's bills, electricity, telephone for £425—all discovered unpaid in Massingham's desk. I want those settled up. They're all final reminders. And the loan to the firm must be paid off as soon as possible.'

I felt icy cold. I wasn't going to cry, I wasn't. I dug my nails into the palms of my hands.

Gareth walked down the table until he was standing over me. Against my will, I looked up. His eyes were as hard and as black as the coal his forefathers had hewn from the mines. In them I could read only hatred and utter contempt, as though he was at last avenging himself for all the wilful havoc I'd created in the past, for breaking up Cathie and Tod, for jeopardizing Gussie and Jeremy.

'You're nothing but a bloody parasite,' he said softly. 'I'm going to make you sweat, beauty. No more helping yourself to everyone's money and their men too. The party's over now. You're going to get a job and do an honest day's work·like everyone else.'

I couldn't look away. I sat there, hypnotized like a rabbit by headlights.

'As your creditor,' he went on, 'I'd quite like to know when you're going to pay up.'

'I'll get it next week,' I whispered.

'How?'

'I'll sell shares.'

He looked at me pityingly.

'Can't you get it into your thick head that unless I can put a bomb under them Seaford-Brennen aren't worth a bean any more? We've also had enquiries from the Inland Revenue; you owe them a bit of bread too.'

The Debtor's Prison loomed. I gripped the edge of the table with my fingers. Then I lost my temper.

'You bloody upstart,' I howled. 'You smug, fat, Welsh prude, walking in here and playing God. Well God's got a great deal more style than you. You're nothing but a bully and a thug. They'll all resign here if you go on humiliating them. See if they don't, and then you'll look bloody silly after all your protestations about waving a fairy wand, and turning us into a miracle of the eighties. God, I loathe you, loathe you.' My voice was rising to a scream now. 'Marching in here, humiliating Xander and Tommy Lloyd, with that fat slob Ricky lapping it all up.'

I paused, my breath coming in great sobs. Then suddenly something snapped outside me. It was my bra strap, beastly disloyal thing. I felt my right tit plummet. Gareth looked at me for a second, then started to laugh.

'You should go on the stage, Octavia; you're utterly wasted on real life,' he said. 'Why not pop down to Billingsgate? I'm sure they'd sign you up as a fishwife.'

'Don't bug me,' I screamed, and groping behind me, gathered up a cut glass ash tray and was just about to smash it in his face when he grabbed my wrist.

'Don't be silly,' he snapped. 'You can't afford to be done for assault as well. Go on, drop it, *drop* it.'

I loosened my fingers; the ashtray fell with a thud on the carpet.

I slumped into a chair, trembling violently. Gareth gave me a cigarette and lit it for me.

'I'll pay it all back,' I muttered, through gritted teeth. 'If I do some modelling I can make that kind of bread in six months.'

'Things have changed, beauty. You can't just swan back to work and pull in ten grand a year. There isn't the work about. You're twenty-six now, not seventeen, and it shows. Anyway, you haven't the discipline to cope with full-time modelling, and it won't do you any good gazing into the camera hour after hour; you'd just get more narcissistic than ever. For Christ's sake get a job where you can use your brain.'

My mind was running round like a spider in a filling-up bath, trying to think of a crushing enough reply. I was saved by the belle—the luscious Mrs. Smith walking in with three cups of coffee. She put one down beside me.

'I don't want any,' I said icily.

'Oh grow up,' said Gareth. 'If you give Annabel a ring she'll help you to get a job and find you somewhere to live.'

I got to my feet.

'She's the last person I'd accept help from,' I said haughtily, preparing to sweep out. But it is very difficult to make a dignified exit with only one bra strap, particularly if one trips over

Mrs. Smith's strategically placed briefcase on the way.

'I expect Annabel's even got a safety pin in her bag, if you ask her nicely,' said Gareth.

I gave a sob and fled from the room.

16

From that moment I was in a dumb blind fury. The only thing that mattered was to pay Seaford-Brennen back, and prove to Gareth and that over-scented fox, Mrs. Smith, that I was quite capable of getting a job and fending for myself.

I went out next day and sold all my jewellery. Most of it, apart from my grandmother's pearls, had been given me by boyfriends. They had been very generous. I got £9,000 for the lot—times were terrible, said the jeweller but at least that would quieten the income tax people for a bit, and pay off the telephone and the housekeeping bills. A woman from a chic second-hand-clothes shop came and bought most of my wardrobe for £600: it must have cost ten times that originally. As she rummaged through my wardrobe I felt she was flaying me alive and rubbing in salt as well. I only kept a handful of dresses I was fond of. There were also a few bits of furniture of my own, the Cotman Xander had given me for my 21st and the picture of the Garden of Eden over the bed. Everything else belonged to the firm.

In the evening Xander rang:

'Sweetheart, are you all right? I meant to ring you yesterday but I passed out cold. And there hasn't been a minute today. How was your session with Gareth?'

'You could hardly say it was riotous,' I said. 'No one put on paper hats. How did you get on this morning?'

'Well that wasn't exactly riotous either. He certainly knows how to kick a chap when he's down. I thought about resigning —then I thought why not stick around and see if he can put us on the map again. He is quite impressive, isn't he?'

'*Oppressive*, certainly.'

'Well tell it not in Gath or the Clermont, or anywhere else,' said Xander. 'But I must confess I do rather like him; he's so unashamedly butch.'

'Et tu Brute,' I said. 'Look, how soon can I put my two decent pictures up for auction at Sotheby's?'

'About a couple of months; but you can't sell pictures—it's blasphemy.'

It took a long time to persuade him I had to.

I spent the next week in consultation with bank managers, accountants, tax people, until I came to the final realization that there was nothing left. I had even buried my pride and written to my mother, but got a gin-splashed letter by return saying she had money troubles of her own and couldn't help.

'You can't get your thieving hands on the family money either,' she had ended with satisfaction. 'It's all in trust for Xander's children, and yours, if you have any.' The only answer seemed to be to get pregnant.

When everything was added up I still owed the tax people a couple of grand, and Seaford-Brennen's £3,400. Both said, with great condescension, that they would give me time to pay.

The heatwave moved into its sixth week. Every news bulletin urged people to save water, and warned of the possibilities of a drought. Cattle were being boxed across the country to less parched areas. In the suffocating, airless heat, I tramped the London streets looking for work and a place to live. I never believed how tough it would be.

Just because one doting ex-lover, who'd put up with all my tantrums and unpunctuality, had directed me through the Revson commercial, I was convinced I could swan into acting and modelling jobs. But I found that Equity had clamped down in the past two years, so I couldn't get film or television commercial work, even if ten million starving out-of-work actresses hadn't been after each job anyway. Modelling was even more disastrous. I went to several auditions and was turned down. I seemed to have lost my sparkle. Gareth's words about not being seventeen anymore, and it showing, kept ringing in my ears. The first photographer who booked me for a job refused to use me because I arrived an hour late. The second kept me sweltering for four hours modelling fur coats, expecting me to behave like a perfectly schooled clothes horse, then threw me out when I started arguing. The third sacked me because I took too long to change my make-up. I moved to another agency, and botched up two more jobs. After that one of the gossip columns printed a bitchy piece about my inability to settle down to anything, and as a result no one was prepared to give me work. Gareth was right anyway—it *was* no cure for a broken heart, gazing into the lens of a camera all day.

I tried a secretarial agency. I asked them what they could offer me. What could I offer them, they answered. Gradually I realized that I was equipped for absolutely nothing. I took a job as a filing clerk in the city. Another catastrophe—within two days I'd completely fouled up the firm's filing system. Next the agency sent me to a job as a receptionist.

'All you have to do, Miss Brennen, is to look pleasant and direct people to the right floor.'

I thought I was doing all right, but after three days the Personnel woman sent for me.

'Receptionists are supposed to be friendly, helpful people. After all, they are the first impression a visitor gets of the company. I'm afraid you're too arrogant, Miss Brennen; you can't look down your nose at people in this day and age. Everyone agrees you've got an unfortunate manner.'

Unfortunate manor—it sounded like a stately home with dry rot. It was a few seconds before I realized she was giving me the boot. The third job I went to, I smiled and smiled until my jaw ached. I lasted till Thursday; then someone told me I had to man the switchboard. No switchboard was ever unmanned faster. After I'd cut off the managing director and his mistress twice, and the sales manager's deal-clinching call to Nigeria for the fourth time a senior secretary with blue hair and a bright red face came down and screamed at me. My nerves in shreds, I screamed back. When I got my first pay packet on Friday morning, it also contained my notice.

Which, all in all, was great on character building but not too hot for morale. One of the bitterest lessons I also learnt was that beauty is largely a matter of time and money. In the old days when I could sleep in until lunchtime, and spend all afternoon sunbathing or slapping on face cream, filing my nails and getting ready to go on the town, it was easy to look good. But now, having to get up at eight o'clock to get to an office by nine-thirty, punched and pummelled to death by commuters on the tube, scurrying round all day with not a moment to do one's face, not getting home till seven absolutely knackered, it was a very different proposition. I lost another seven pounds and all my selfconfidence; for the first time in my life I walked down the street and no one turned their heads to look at me. In a way it was rather a relief.

After the secretarial agency gave me up, I rang up a few old friends who owned boutiques. Their reactions were all the same. They were either laying off staff, or told me kindly that their sort of work would bore me to death, which really meant they thought I was totally unreliable.

In the evenings I went and looked for flats which was even more depressing. Living on my own, I couldn't afford any-where remotely reasonable, and in my present mood I couldn't bear to share with other girls. All that cooking scrambled eggs, knickers dripping over the bath, and shrieking with laughter over last night's exploits. It wasn't just that I couldn't face new people, I was feeling so low I couldn't believe they'd put up with me.

I was also fast running out of Valium—only six left, not even enough for an overdose. I couldn't go to my doctor; I owed him too much money. At night I didn't sleep, tossing and turn-ing, eating my heart out for Gareth, worrying about leaving my darling flat, my only refuge. At the back of my mind, flickering like a snake's tongue, was the thought of Andreas Katz. If I took up his modelling offer, it would get me off the hook, but I knew once Andreas had something on me, or in this case, everything off me, I'd never escape. I'd be sucked down to damnation like a quicksand. Even Xander had deserted me; he hadn't called me for days. Gareth must be working the pants off him.

I was due to move out on the Saturday. The Thursday before, I sat, surrounded by suitcases, poring over the *Evening Standard*, trying not to cry, and wondering whether 'Bedsitter in Muswell Hill with lively family, £15 a week, some baby sitting in return' was worth investigation, when the telephone rang. I pounced on it like a cat. I still couldn't cure myself of the blind hope it might be Gareth. But it was only Lorna asking if she could come and stay the night. It was the last thing I wanted, but I had a masochistic desire to find out what Gareth was up to.

'You'll have to camp,' I said, 'I'm moving out the day after tomorrow.'

'Well, if it's not too much bother, I'd so adore to see you again.'

She arrived about six o'clock in a flurry of parcels and suitcases.

'I've gone mad buying sexy clothes,' were her first words. 'Gareth's taking me out tonight.'

I couldn't stand it, sitting in the flat and seeing her get all scented and beautiful for him.

I showed her to her room and then went into my bedroom and telephoned my ex-boyfriend, Charlie, and asked him to take me out.

He was enchanted. 'God, it's great to hear you baby. Mountain's come to Mahomet at last. I won a monkey at poker last night so we can go anywhere you want. I'll pick you up about nine.'

'Can't you get here any earlier?'

'I'll try, sweetheart.'

I wandered along to Lorna's bedroom. She was trying on a new orange dress she'd just bought.

'Do you think Gareth will like me in this?' she said, craning her neck to see her back in the mirror.

'Yes,' I said truthfully. 'You look ravishing. I'm going out too by the way, at about nine.'

'Oh, Gareth's coming at a quarter to, so you should see him.'

While she was in the bath, the telephone rang. Trembling, I picked up the receiver. Somehow I knew it was going to be Gareth.

'Lorna's in the bath,' I said quickly. 'Can I give her a message?'

'Yeah, tell her I'll be a bit late, around nine-thirty.'

'All right,' I said.

'How are you?' he asked brusquely.

'I'm fine,' I stammered. 'And you?'

'Tired, I've been working too hard. I'm off to the Middle East with your brother next week, which should be enlightening if nothing else. Have you found somewhere to live?'

'Yes thanks,' I said. 'I'm moving out tomorrow.'

'What about a job?'

'That's fine too. I must go,' I went on, fighting back the tears. 'I've got so much to do. Goodbye.' And I put down the receiver.

I can't stand it, I can't stand it, I thought in agony.

Lorna walked in, wrapped in a towel, pink from her bath.

'Oh I feel so much better. I used your Badedas. I hope you don't mind.'

'That was Gareth,' I said. 'He's going to be late—about nine-thirty.'

'Oh goodee, that'll give me more time to tart myself up.'

Suddenly she looked at me.

'Octavia, you look awfully pale. Are you all right?'

Tears, embarrassingly hot and prickly, rose to my ears. I began to laugh, gasped hysterically, and then burst into tears.

'Octavia! Oh poor love, what is it?'

'N-nothing. Everything,' I couldn't stop now.

'What's wrong? Please tell me.'

'Oh, the usual thing.'

'You're mad for someone?'

'Yes.'

'Well you're so stunning, he must be mad for you.'

'He isn't. He hardly knows I exist.'

'He couldn't know you properly then. Here, take my handkerchief.'

'I'd better go and get ready,' I said. 'I've got to go out in a minute.'

I put on a black trouser suit with a high mandarin collar and huge floppy trousers. It hung off me. I tied my hair back with a black bow. Were those dry lips and red swollen eyes really mine? Charlie wouldn't recognize me.

Lorna answered the door when he arrived. She came rushing into my bedroom.

'He's *absolutely* gorgeous. The campest thing I've ever seen,' she said excitedly. 'I'm not surprised you're wild about him.'

It was too much effort to explain to her he wasn't the one.

'Can you give him a drink?' I said. 'I'll be out in a minute.'

I hung around, fiddling with my make-up, trying to summon up enough courage to face him. I'd lost all my confidence. Finally I realized if I didn't get a move on I'd go slap into Gareth.

Charlie looked exquisite, and to me, absurd. He had already helped himself to a second whisky and was settling down on the sofa to chat up Lorna.

He got to his feet when I came in and pecked me on the cheek.

'Hullo baby. Playing it in the minor key for a change,' he said, taking in the black suit, the dark glasses, the drawnback hair. 'I like it, it's great.'

'Shall we go?' I said, going towards the door.

'Already?' said Charlie. 'I haven't finished my drink.'

'I want to go now,' I snapped.

'The lady seems to be in a hurry, so I'll bid you goodnight,' said Charlie, theatrically, bowing from the waist to Lorna. 'I hope you'll come into the shop one day now you're in London.'

'You've got a key, haven't you?' I said to her. 'Have a good evening. I'll see you in the morning.'

'Hey, what's bitten you?' said Charlie, as we went down in the lift.

It was a hideous evening. In three short weeks I seemed to have grown a world apart from Charlie and his flash trendy friends, waiting round in Tramps all night for something to happen, only interested in being the first ones to latch on to the latest fad. Suddenly their values seemed completely dislocated.

We went to Annabel's and I couldn't stand it, then we moved on to the Dumbbells, then on to somewhere else and somewhere else. Finally Charlie took me back to his flat and we played records.

I have to hand it to Charlie; he seemed to realize instinctively that I was at suicide level and didn't attempt to pounce on me in his usual fashion. Perhaps it had something to do with his having a new girlfriend who was off modelling in Stockholm for a couple of days. I looked at my watch. It was three o'clock.

'What's the matter baby?' he asked. 'Have you fallen for some bloke at last? I've never seen you so *piano*, you're not even bitching how bored you are by everything this evening. You look different too.'

He took off my dark glasses.

'Boy; you do look different. I must say I rather go for the Ave Maria look.'

It would have helped if I could have cried on his shoulder, but I'd gone beyond that stage now, I was just numb with misery.

'Take me home, please Charlie,' I said.

Next day, life picked up about half an inch. For an hour I endured the torture of listening to Lorna babbling on at breakfast about the marvellous time she'd had with Gareth.

'After dinner, we went up to the top of the Hilton for a

147

drink, and looked out over the whole of London, it was so romantic,' she said, helping herself to a third piece of toast and marmalade. Her mascara was still smudged under her eyes. I hoped it wasn't sex that had given her such an appetite.

Then she started to ask me awkward questions about the new job I'd lied to Gareth that I'd got.

'It's in Knightsbridge,' I said.

'Well you must give me the telephone number because you'll be moving out of here.'

'I'll be travelling a lot,' I said hastily. 'And they're always a bit dodgy about personal calls to start off with. I'll write and tell you.'

'It sounds marvellous,' said Lorna, selecting a banana. 'But if by chance it doesn't work out, Gareth says there's a marvellous new agency started up in Albemarle Street called Square Peg. They specialize in placing people who want to branch out in completely new fields.'

'I'll take the address just in case,' I said.

As soon as she'd gone, pleading with me to come and spend the weekend soon, I had a bath, painted my face with great care, took my last two Valium, and set out for Square Peg. They turned out to be very friendly and businesslike, and dispatched me straightaway to a public relations firm in the City.

The firm's offices were scruffy, untidy, and terribly hot. The secretary who welcomed me looked tired out, and her hair needed washing, but she gave me the sort of smile that all those personnel bitches I'd worked for were always banging on about.

'It's been a hell of a week,' she said. 'The air conditioning's broken and the heat's been terrible. It's crazy hard work here, but it's fun.'

The boss was a small dark Jew called Jakey Bartholomew, who seemed to burn with energy. His foxy, brown eyes shone with intelligence behind horn-rimmed spectacles. He had to lift a lot of files, a box of pork chops, and a huge cutout cardboard of a pig off a chair before I could sit down.

'We've just landed the Pig Industry account,' he said grinning. 'I'm trying to persuade them to produce kosher pork.

We've been going for nine months now, and we're taking on new business all the time because we provide the goods on a shoestring. Do you know anything about public relations?'

'No,' I said.

'Just as well. You haven't had time to pick up any bad habits.' He ripped open a couple of beer cans and gave me one.

'We're a small outfit, only ten people in the firm, and we can't afford passengers. We need a girl Friday—you can see this place is in shit order—to keep it tidy, make decent coffee, and chat up the clients when they come. Then you'd have to do things like putting press releases into envelopes, taking them to the post, organizing press parties, and probably writing the odd release. It's very menial work.'

'I don't care,' I said, trying to keep the quiver of desperation out of my voice. 'I'll do anything.'

'If you're good we'll promote you very fast.'

Suddenly he grinned, reminding me of Gareth.

'All right, you're on, baby. Go along to the accounts department in a minute and get your P.45 sorted out. We'll start you on a three months trial on Monday.'

I couldn't believe my luck; I hardly concentrated as we discussed hours and salaries, and he told me a bit more about the firm. He was very forceful. It was only when I stood up to go that I realized I was about four inches taller than he was.

'The agency was right,' he said. 'They insisted you were a very classy looking dame.'

I didn't remember the agency saying any such thing when they telephoned through. They must have rung again after I'd left.

I then took a long 22 bus ride out to Putney where the *Evening Standard* had advertised a room to let. Everywhere I could see the ravages of the drought, great patches of black burnt grass, flowers gasping with thirst in dried-up gardens. As I got off the bus, a fire engine charged past, clanging noisily. Although it was only the end of July, a bonfire smell of autumn filled my nostrils.

The house was large and Victorian on the edge of the

common, the front rooms darkened by a huge chestnut tree. A stocky woman answered the door. She had a tough face like dried out roast beef, and muddy, mottled knees. She was wearing a flowered sleeveless dress that rucked over her large hips. Rose petals in her iron grey hair gave her an incongruously festive look. At present she was more interested in stopping several dogs escaping than letting me in.

'I've come about the room,' I said.

'Oh,' she said, looking slightly more amiable. 'I'm Mrs. Lonsdale-Taylor. Come in, sorry to look such a mess, I've been gardening. Come here Monkey,' she bellowed to a small brown mongrel who was trying to lick my hand.

'Mind the loose rod,' she said as we climbed the stairs. In front of me her sturdy red legs went into her shoes without the intervention of ankles. Her voice was incredibly put on. I was sure she'd double-barrelled the Lonsdale and Taylor herself.

The room was at the top of the house; the sofa clashed with the wallpaper, the brass bed creaked when I sat on it, rush matting hardly covered the black scratched floorboards. On the wall were framed photographs cut out from magazines and stuck on cardboard. The curtains hung a foot above the floor like midi skirts. It would be a cold and cheerless room in winter.

I looked outside. In spite of the drought Mrs. Lonsdale-Taylor had been taking great care of her garden. The mingled scent of stocks, clove carnations and a honeysuckle, which hung in great honey-coloured ramparts round the window, drifted towards me. A white cat emerged from a forest of dark blue delphiniums and, avoiding the sprinkler that was shooting its rainbow jets over the green lawn, walked towards the house at a leisurely pace. It was incredibly quiet.

'It's beautiful here,' I said. 'You're lucky to be so countrified living so near London.'

I bent to stroke the little brown mongrel who'd followed us upstairs. He wagged his tail and put both his paws up on my waist.

'Get down, Monkey,' said Mrs. Lonsdale-Taylor, aiming a

kick at him. 'He was my late husband's dog, I've never really taken to him. My husband passed on last year, or I wouldn't be taking people in.'

'Of course not,' I murmured.

'I prefer a pedigree dog myself,' she said, wiping her nose with her hand, and leaving a moustache of earth on her upper lip.

'Well, if you like the room, it's £15 a week all in, but you've got to pay for your own telephone. I've installed a 'phone box downstairs. You can use the kitchen when I'm not using it, as long as you clear up afterwards, but no food in the bedroom. I don't mind you having friends in if they behave themselves, but no gramophones, or young gentlemen after nine o'clock. And I'd like the first month's rent when you arrive. I like to get these things straight.'

17

Looking back, I shall never know how I got through the next few weeks. I hadn't realized that the journey from Putney to the city would take two hours in the rush-hour, or in this heat, the bus would be like a Turkish bath. My second day working for Jakey Bartholomew I didn't get in till quarter to ten, and received such a bawling out I thought I'd blown the whole thing. But gradually as the days passed I began to pick up the job. I learnt to work the switchboard and skim the papers for anything important and stick press cuttings into a scrap book. The work was so menial that sometimes I did scream. But Jakey was a hard taskmaster, and came down on any displays of sulks or ill-temper like a ton of concrete slabs. In the same way, he picked me up for any stupid mistakes.

Gradually too, I got to know the other girls in the office, and learnt to grumble with them about the lateness of the second post, and the failure of the roller towel in the lavatory, and have long discussions about Miss Selfridges and eye make-up. The days were made bearable by little unimportant victories— one of the typists asking me to go to the cinema; Miss Parkside, the office crone, inviting me to supper at her flat in Peckham; a client ringing up asking if I could be spared to show some V.I.P. Germans round London.

I soon discovered, however, that I'd never be able to pay Seaford-Brennen back on my present salary, so I took another job waitressing in Putney High Street. Here, for six nights a week, and at lunchtime on Saturdays, I worked my guts out, earning £40 a week by looking pleasant when drunken customers pinched my bottom, or bollocked me because the chef had had a row with his boyfriend and forgotten to put any salt in the Chicken Marengo. At the end of each week I sent my £40 salary in a registered envelope to Mrs. Smith, and received a polite acknowledgement. Gareth was still in the Middle East with Xander so at least I didn't worry all day about bumping into him.

Every night I fell into bed long after midnight, too knackered to allow myself more than a second to dream about him. But his face still haunted my dreams and every morning I would wake up crying, with the sun beating through the thin curtains, and the little mongrel Monkey, curled up on my bed, looking at me with sorrowful dark eyes, trying to lick away my tears. He was a great comfort. I couldn't understand why Mrs. Lonsdale-Taylor preferred her fat Pekineses. I realized now how much my mother had deprived me of, never letting me have animals.

August gave way to September; the drought grew worse; it hadn't rained for three months; the common was like a cinder; the leaves on the chestnut tree shrivelled and turned brown. People were ordered not to use their hose-pipes. Mrs. L-T panted back and forth with buckets of water, grumbling.

On the Tuesday of my eighth week, Jakey Bartholomew sent

152

for me. I went in quaking.

'You can't send this out,' he said.

He handed me a photograph of a girl with very elaborate frizzled curls, one of the dreadful styles created by our hair-dressing client, Roger of Kensington. Turning it over I saw I'd captioned it:

'Sweet and sour pigs trotters'—one of the Pig Industry's equally dreadful recipes.

'Oh God, I'm sorry,' I said.

Jakey started to laugh.

'I thought it was quite funny. Have a beer, get one out of the fridge.'

I helped myself and sat down.

Jakey leaned back. 'Our advertising associates want to borrow your legs on Friday week.'

'They what?'

'They're pitching for a stocking account. All the guys reckon you've got the best pair of legs in either office. They want you to model the tights for them during the presentation.'

I felt myself blushing scarlet. I never realized any of the men in the office had even noticed me; they'd certainly kept their distance.

'They want to take some photographs this afternoon,' said Jakey, 'and get them blown up by next week.' I said that was O.K. by me. 'If they land the account, we'll probably get the P.R. side. And if the client likes the idea, they may use you in ads, which could make you quite a lot of bread.'

'Thank you so much,' I stammered. I felt I had conquered Everest.

'Are you feeling all right?' he said, as I went out. 'You're looking knackered.'

'I'm fine,' I said quickly.

'Well bring me the Roger of Kensington file then.'

He was right of course. Gradually I was coming apart at the seams. In the last week or so I had noticed a growing inability in myself to make decisions, even small ones. The problem of where to find the file suddenly began to swell like a balloon in my head. The familiar panic began to surge inside me. I'm going crazy, I whimpered. I put my hands on my forehead and waited. Keep calm, it'll go in a minute, don't panic.

I felt as if I were trying to get out of a dark slimy cavern, and my nails kept grating down the inside. My mind raced from one fear to the other, in search of a grip to secure myself from the blind horror that swirled around me. I leant against the wall, trying to take deep breaths, praying no one would come out into the passage. Gradually the panic ebbed away. I went into the general office. It was empty. With shaking hands I dialled the number of the psychiatrist who'd been recommended to me in the old days. I made an appointment for Thursday lunchtime.

The first visit wasn't a conspicuous success. The analyst was middle-aged, handsome, well-dressed, with teeth as white as his shirt-cuffs, a soothing deliberate manner, and a photograph of a beautiful wife and child on the desk. I was too uptight to tell him very much, but he gave me enough tranquillizers to last a week, on condition that I returned again next Thursday lunchtime.

'It's very kind, but I can't afford it,' I muttered.

I felt a totally doglike gratitude when he waved my protestations airily away and said:

'Don't give it a thought, Miss Brennen. In exceptional circumstances I take National Health patients, and your case interests me very much.'

The tranquillizers got me through another week. My legs were photographed in every conceivable type of stocking, and the advertising department professed themselves delighted with the result.

The following Thursday morning, just as I was setting out for the doctor, Xander rang, just back from the Middle East, and absolutely raving over his trip. He and Gareth had pulled off some fantastic deals he said, and Gareth was a star.

'I simply adore him,' he went on. 'I'm thinking of divorcing Pammie and asking him to wait for me, and darling, he can sell *absolutely anything*, even a pregnant rabbit to an

Australian sheep farmer, if he felt so inclined. We had a terrible time to begin with. I didn't realize the Middle East was dry. For twenty-four hours we didn't have a drink, then the pink elephants started trooping into my bedroom, and Gareth had a quiet word with the resident Sheik. From then on we had whisky pouring out of our ears.'

'Was it terribly hot?' I said.

'Terrible, and if I see another belly dancer, I'll go bananas.'

'Did Gareth have lots of birds out there?' I said, suddenly feeling my voice coming out like a ventriloquist's dummy.

'No, actually he didn't. I think he's got some bird in England he's hooked on.'

'Any idea who?'

'Well, this ravishing redhead met him at the airport, bubbling over with excitement, flinging her arms round him.'

'Mrs. Smith?' I said in a frozen whisper.

'No, much younger. Laura, I think she was called.'

'Lorna Hamilton?'

'Yes, that's it. Gareth was supposed to be giving me a lift into London, but I left them to it.'

Almost sleep-walking, I got myself to the analyst. On the way I passed a church; the gutter outside was choked with confetti. Gareth and Lorna, Gareth and Lorna, a voice intoned inside me—they sounded like a couple by Tennyson.

The analyst had darkened his waiting room. After the searching sunlight it was beautifully cool. His receptionist got me a glass of iced water, and then I heard him telling her to go to lunch. I lay down on the grey velvet sofa. This time I found myself able to talk. I didn't tell him about Gareth, but raved on about my childhood.

'I wasn't allowed to be loving as a child,' I sobbed. 'My mother didn't love me. She never kissed me goodnight or tucked me up. Neither of my parents loved me, they fought like cats to have custody of my brother, Xander, but they fought equally hard not to have me . . .'

'Go on,' said the analyst noncommitally. I could feel his pale

155

blue eyes watching me, smell the lavender tang of his after-shave.

'I know what happens to people who aren't loved enough,' I went on. 'They just close up, and love or hate themselves too much. They're incapable of getting it together with anyone else . . .'

After three-quarters of an hour of my ramblings, he glanced at his watch.

I got up to go.

'I'm sorry, I must have bored you to death. You can't possibly put me on the National Health.'

'I thought we'd dispensed with all that,' he said gently. 'You'll come again next week?'

'Oh please, if you can spare the time.'

He scribbled out a prescription. 'Here's another week's supply of Valium.'

He turned towards me, the prescription suddenly trembling in his hand. He was trying to smile; his blue eyes glazed, his face pale, he was sweating and there was a tic in his cheek. Then he walked round the table, stood in front of me and put a wet hand on my arm.

'I was wondering,' he said, that tic was going again, 'if I might see you—outside consulting hours. I am sure I could show you there was no need to be so lonely.'

Behind him, smiling sunnily, was the photograph of his wife and children. I had trusted him implicitly.

'I d-don't think it'd be very wise,' I said, backing away from him, 'I've never found married men very satisfactory.'

I wrenched open the door behind me, amazed to find it unlocked. I saw fear start in his eyes, the Medical Council passing judgment. Then he squared his shoulders.

'Of course,' he pressed the bell on the desk, magicking up the instant receptionist to show me out.

I ran down the street prescriptionless and sobbed helplessly in the nearest garden square.

By some miracle I got back to the office just before Miss Parkside, the office crone. She arrived grumbling that she couldn't find a 16 size skirt to fit her anymore, and brandishing a large Fuller's cake to distract everyone's attention from her lateness.

'I suppose I ought to have worn my all in one,' she said, plunging a knife into the hard white icing, 'but it's too hot in this weather. It must be well up in the nineties. Come on, Octavia, you need feeding up.'

She handed me an enormous piece. In order to save money, I'd trained myself to go without lunch and breakfast. I usually had something to eat free in the evening at the restaurant while I was waitressing. Every mouthful of the cake seemed like sand in my throat. All the typists looked sympathetically at my reddened eyes, but said nothing.

My task for the afternoon was to ring up the papers and chase them to come to a press preview the next morning. I found it distasteful and embarrassing. In the middle Xander suddenly rang me. He sounded drunk.

'I know you don't like personal calls, darling, but this is a very special one. You're going to be an aunt.'

'A what?'

'An Aunt! Pammie's pregnant.'

I gave a scream of delight that must have echoed through the whole building.

'Oh Xander, are you sure?'

'Quite, quite sure, she's even being sick, poor darling.'

'How long's she known?'

'Well, just after I went to the Middle East, but she wanted to be quite sure before she told anyone.'

I'd never known him so chipper.

'Good old Pammie, isn't it marvellous,' he went on, 'Ricky rang me up just now and was so nice, he even congratulated me about work, said the Middle East trip had been a great coup. Look, darling, I mustn't keep you, I know you're busy, but come over and celebrate at the weekend.'

I put the telephone down feeling utterly depressed. I knew I ought to be delighted, but all I could think was Xander was getting so far ahead of me in life, with a job that was going well,

157

and a baby on the way. I felt sick with jealousy. I wanted a baby of my own. Listlessly I finished making my telephone calls, and started stapling press releases together for the preview tomorrow. The afternoon sun was blazing through the window. I could feel the sweat running down my back. Miss Parkside and the typists had already started grumbling about the prospects of the journey home.

The telephone went again. Miss Parkside picked it up.

'For you,' she said, disapprovingly. 'Make it snappy.'

It was Lorna. I could recognize the breathless, bubbling schoolgirl voice anywhere. This time she was jibbering with excitement and embarrassment.

'Octavia, I must see you.'

I felt my hands wet on the telephone.

'Where are you?' I said.

'At home.'

Memories came flooding back, the white house deep in the cherry orchards, Gareth beating the hell out of me, then putting me to bed, Jeremy trying to rape me.

'But I'm coming to London tomorrow,' she went on. 'Could we have lunch, I've got something I must tell you.'

'Nice or nasty?' I asked.

'Well, heaven for me, but I'm not sure . . .' her voice trailed off.

'Tell it to me now.'

'I can't, I'm in such a muddle,' she said. 'Please, let's meet for lunch. I'll come and pick you up.'

'I've got a very heavy day.'

'You can slip out just for a drink. I'll pick you up at one o'clock. And please Octavia, don't, don't be furious with me.'

The telephone went dead. I stood for a second, then just made the loo in time, and threw up all the Fuller's cake. For a second I crouched, wracked by retching and sobbing. So it *was* true about Gareth and Lorna, it must be what she was trying to tell me. With agonizing slowness, I pulled myself together. You must finish those press releases, I said over and over again, as though it was really me that needed stapling together. I splashed water over my face and rinsed out my mouth. God, I looked terrible. My suntan had turned yellow. My eyes were red and puffy. My hair, filthy and dark mouse at the roots because I couldn't afford to have it re-streaked, was bleached like straw at the ends. One of the secretaries poked her head round the door.

'Parkside's on the warpath,' she said. 'Some V.I.P.'s just arrived. Can you make him a cup of coffee and take it into Jakey's office?'

I couldn't find my dark glasses. The wretched V.I.P. would have to put up with reddened eyes. I knocked on Jakey's door and walked into his office. The next moment the cup of coffee had crashed to the ground, for sitting behind the desk was Gareth. He leapt to his feet.

'Are you O.K. lovely? You haven't burnt yourself?'

'I'm fine,' I muttered. 'But it'll ruin the carpet.'

I grabbed a drying-cloth that was lying on top of the fridge and, kneeling down, started frenziedly mopping up the coffee. Anything for Gareth not to get a glimpse of my face. I hadn't seen him for over two months; he'd have a fit to catch me looking so awful.'

'Leave it,' he said. 'It'll dry in a minute.'

He put a hand under my elbow and pulled me to my feet.

'I'll get you another cup of coffee,' I said, making a bolt for the door.

But he got there first, standing in front of me, shutting the door firmly. As usual his presence made the room shrink.

'Sit down,' he said, tipping a pile of files off a chair. 'I want to talk to you.'

'What are you doing here anyway?' I said. I still hadn't looked him in the eyes.

'Visiting my old mate Jakey Bartholomew.'

'You know him?' I said sharply. 'But I didn't, I mean . . .'

'You should read your own company notepaper,' said Gareth. He handed me a sheet that was lying on Jakey's desk. Sure enough in the middle of the list of directors was printed G. Llewellyn.

'T-then you fiddled me this job,' I blurted out. 'I thought I g-got it on my own . . .'

'Merits, yes of course you did,' he said gently. 'Jakey'd have never employed you if he hadn't liked you.' He held up one of the blown-up photographs of my legs.

'I must say I like these. I'd recognize those pins anywhere.'

Everything was moving too fast for me. I was trying to work out what influence Gareth must have had over my working at Bartholomews.

'How are you enjoying it anyway?' he said.

'It's fine. How was the Middle East trip?'

'Hell,' said Gareth. 'And bloody hot and exhausting. Your brother was the only redeeming feature.'

'He's nice, isn't he?'

'He overreached himself one night. He charmed one sheik so much that later the sheik insisted that only Xander should have the culinary *piece de resistance* at dinner.'

'What was it?' I said.

'A sheep's eyeball,' said Gareth.

I started to giggle.

'He's over the moon about the baby,' I said, trying to keep the trace of wistfulness out of my voice.

'Yep, it's a good thing. It'll patch up things between him and Ricky, too.'

There was a pause. The room was suffocatingly hot. I still hadn't looked at him. A schoolgirl embarking on her first love affair couldn't have behaved with more gaucheness. I felt hollow with longing and misery.

'It's very hot isn't it?' I said.

'Very,' said Gareth.

This wasn't getting us very far. I got to my feet, edging towards the door.

'I must get you some coffee.'

'I don't want any.'

'I-I've got some work I've got to finish.'

He followed me into the general office, passing Miss Parkside on the way out, bearing her floral sponge-bag off to the Ladies.

'It's going-home time,' he said.

'I've got to finish these,' I said, picking a page off the four separate piles of paper until they shook in my hand as though they were being fluttered by an electric fan.

Gareth looked at me for a minute.

'You're getting them all out of order,' he said, taking them from me, and restacking them. He shoved them between the stapler and banged it down with one hand. Nothing happened.

'Bloody thing's run out,' he said. 'Come on, you can do them in the morning. I'll buy you a drink.'

The bar was crowded with commuters who couldn't face the journey home yet. Gareth found me a bar stool, I curled my feet round one of the legs, trying to control the hammering in my heart. In a minute I knew I'd wake up from a dream, and be crying back in bed in Putney. He handed me a gin and tonic and shot soda into his whisky. I took a slug of my drink at once, gripping it with both hands to stop them shaking.

I glanced up at the smoked mirror behind the bar; my eyes met Gareth's. For a second we gazed at each other with a steady fascination, as though we were two quite different people, in another world for the first time. I felt if his sleeve touched mine the whole bar would burst into flames.

I tugged my eyes away and took another gulp.

'You've lost a lot of weight,' he said.

'Have I?'

'Too much.'

'It's the heat.'

He glanced at the beige sausage rolls and curling sandwiches in the glass case.

'D'you want something now?'

I shook my head. A fire engine clanged past the door, followed by another.

'D'you think it'll ever rain again?' I said.

I noticed for the first time how tired he looked, the black rings under his eyes, almost as dark as his eyebrows.

'Is Seaford-Brennen too much of a sweat?' I said.

'Well it's not exactly a day trip to Llandudno,' he said.

'Jakey's very pleased with you, by the way.'

I felt myself blushing. 'He is?'

'Yep, and so am I. You haven't just turned over a new leaf, Brennen, it's a bloody great tree.'

He looked at me reflectively for a minute.

'Why have you been crying your eyes out all afternoon?'

I took a hasty swig of my drink, the glass was too deep and it ran all over my face.

'I'm trying to get my head sorted out,' I said, frantically wiping gin away with my sleeve. 'So I started going to a shrink.'

'Jesus, you don't need a shrink.'

'H-he thinks I do. He pounced on me today.'

I started to tremble again. For a moment Gareth's hand tightened on my arm, then he said,

'The bastard. Report him to the medical council.'

'I don't think you can report shrinks, but it was a shock. I sort of trusted him.'

'You give me his name and address, and I'll get him kicked out,' said Gareth. He was really angry. God, he was being so nice, any minute I'd start crying again. I took a bite of my lemon peel.

'Lorna rang me this afternoon,' I said. 'She was in the country.'

Suddenly he looked evasive and shifty. He got out a packet of cigarettes, and when I refused one, lit one for himself.

'She said she had something special to tell me,' I went on, 'but she wouldn't tell me over the telephone in case it upset me.'

Gareth shook his ice round in his glass.

'Do you want another drink?'

I shook my head, the lump was getting bigger and bigger in my throat.

'She sounded over the moon, like Xander,' I continued. 'I guess she was trying to tell me she was getting married.'

'Yep,' said Gareth. 'That's about it.'

'Soon?' I said.

'Pretty soon. Lorna's one of those girls who wants to keep

her virginity for marriage. She's worried she can't hold out much longer.'

'Bully for her,' I whispered.

'She feels terribly guilty,' he went on. 'She's worried stiff about upsetting you, and she knows Hesketh and Bridget are going to say she's too young.'

'You can't win them all,' I said in a choked voice.

'Look Octavia, you're a beautiful, beautiful girl. There are plenty of other guys in the sea, and masses on land for that matter.'

'Sure,' I said numbly, the tears beginning to course down my cheeks.

He took my hand; it was all I could do not to fling myself into his arms.

'I'm really sorry,' he went on. 'Look I've got nothing to do tonight. I'll buy you dinner and we can talk about it.'

'No you won't. It's very kind, but no thank you,' I said, wiping away the tears with the back of my hand. 'I've already got a date,' and breaking away, I slid off the bar stool and fled out of the bar.

'Octavia, wait,' I heard his voice calling after me. Then I plunged down into the Underground.

18

When I got back to Putney, Monkey threw himself on me, yelping with ecstasy, taking my hand in his mouth, and leading me up the path. I found Mrs. Lonsdale-Taylor grumbling about the heat and the greenfly and pouring boiling water on a plague of ants who were threatening to enter the house. The dustmen were on strike and hadn't collected for two weeks; the stench of Jeyes fluid in the dustbins was almost worse than yesterday's smell of rotting food and vegetation.

Mrs. Lonsdale-Taylor straightened up, scarlet in the face.

'There's a young man waiting for you upstairs,' she said with a sniff, 'he says he's your brother.'

I bounded upstairs, I couldn't wait to tell someone how miserable I was. Xander loved Gareth too; he would understand how suicidal I felt. I found him in my bedroom, his face had a luminous sickly tinge, as though he was standing under a green umbrella. A muscle was going in his cheek. The ashtray beside him on the table was piled high with half-smoked cigarettes.

'Thank God you've come,' he said. 'I'm in dead trouble.'

His light brown hair, almost black from sweat, had fallen in a fringe over his forehead, emphasizing the brilliant grey eyes. He looked absurdly young. I ran across the room and put my arms round him.

'What's happened? Tell me. It's not the baby?'

He shook his head.

'I'm sorry,' I said. 'I haven't got anything to drink. Tell me what's the matter.'

'I've got to get £2,000 by tomorrow.'

'God, whatever for?'

'I'm being blackmailed.'

'Then you must go to the police at once.'

'I can't,' he said with a groan. He was near to tears. I realized I was the one who had to stay as calm and cool as a statue.

'You must go to the police; they'll keep your name out of it. What on earth have you done? It can't be *that* bad.'

The door suddenly opened, making us both jump, but it was only Monkey. He trotted over and curled up at Xander's feet. I kicked the door shut.

'Who is it?' I asked.

'It's Guido,' said Xander in a dead voice.

'Guido?'

'The Italian boy, the good-looking one you met that day we had lunch at Freddy's, before you went on the boat with Gareth and Jeremy.'

'Oh yes, I remember,' I said.

'That weekend you were away I refused to go and stay with Ricky and Joan.'

'Yes.'

'I went down to Devon with Guido—to a gay hotel.'

Oh God!

'Well one of his mates turned up, another pretty boy, also Italian, and we all got stoned of course, and started taking polaroid photographs in the bedroom. Some of them went pretty far. Now Guido and his pal want a couple of grand for a start, and if I don't cough up tomorrow, they're going to send the photos to Pammie and Ricky.'

I thought for a minute. The scent of tobacco plants was almost sickening outside. I could hear the outside tap water plummeting into Mrs. L-T's watering can.

'Don't you think Pammie twigged long ago?' I said. 'She's not stupid.'

'She can't admit it, even to herself.'

'Wouldn't it be better to tell her?'

Xander's voice broke. 'Not when she's pregnant. She was so happy about the baby, and suddenly everything's going so well at work, and we're getting on so much better at the moment.'

There was no point in reminding him he'd only been back from the Middle East twenty-four hours.

'Ricky'll throw me out, and so will Pamela, and I know it sounds wet, but I really want that baby. You've got lots of rich friends.'

'What about Gareth?' I said. 'He'll help you.'

'I'm getting on so well with *him* too,' said Xander fretfully.

'If you give in to Guido this time, he'll only be back for more bread in a week or two.'

'If I get a breathing space,' said Xander, 'I can think of a way to hammer him, I just need time. Oh for God's sake Octavia,' his voice rose, almost womanish, 'I've helped you out enough times in the past.'

It was true.

'All right, I'll get you the money,' I said.

'How?'

'I've got a friend who's offered me £1,500 to do some modelling,' I said, 'I guess I can push him up to £2,000.'

As soon as Xander had gone I went out to a telephone box and dialled Andreas's number.

I imagined him pushing aside a blonde, and climbing over a huge pair of tits to answer the telephone.

'Hullo,' said the husky, oily, foreign voice.

'Andreas,' I said. 'This is Octavia.'

There was a pause.

'Octavia Brennen.'

'I know,' he said softly. 'Just let me turn this redhead down. I was expecting a call from you.'

'You were?' I said sharply. 'What d'you mean?'

'Well, the grapevine said you were having rather a lean time, and you'd left the flat. Pity. It was a nice situation, that flat. Anyway, what can I do for you?'

I swallowed. 'Do you remember what you said about photographing me for *Hedonist*?'

'Sure do.' He had difficulty keeping the triumph out of his voice.

'You were talking in terms of £1,500,' I said.

'I must have been crazy.'

'Could you make it £2,000?'

'Inflation's clobbered everyone, baby.'

'Not that much. Your circulation's booming. I read it in *Campaign* last week.'

'Well, if you make yourself available for—er—dinner and other things afterwards, I might consider it.'

He waited. I could almost feel him writhing like a great snake in anticipation. What the hell did it matter? Gareth was caput as far as I was concerned. What did anything matter?

'All right,' I said, 'that would be nice. But can I have the cash tomorrow?'

'Greedy, aren't we? I hope there's nothing the matter with you, Octavia. I've never known you haggle before. Take it or leave it, that's the sort of duchess you always were. I wouldn't like you to be any different. It'd make me think things had a certain impermanence.'

'I need the bread,' I said.

'All right.' His voice suddenly businesslike. 'Cy Markovitz is in London at the moment. I've booked him all day tomorrow. Come along at two.'

In utter misery I realized I would have to cut the presentation. But getting the money for Xander had to be more important than anything else.

'All right,' I said.

He gave me the address and then added softly.

'And don't wear anything tight. We don't want crease marks all over you. Till tomorrow, darling. You won't regret it, I promise you.'

After that I had to go and waitress. When I got home I washed my hair and made pathetic attempts to get my body into some sort of shape to be photographed. I then spent hours writing and tearing up letters of explanation to Jakey. Even the final result didn't satisfy me. I was so much on the blink, I could hardly string a word, let alone a sentence, together and nothing I said could change the fact I was doing the dirty on him. Monkey lay on the bed, dozing, unsettled by the change in routine. Every so often he gave a yawn which turned into a squeaking yelp. I refused to go to bed, it was too hot to sleep anyway, and if I did sleep I would have to wake up and face afresh the truth about Gareth and Lorna.

Nothing—not even the truth—prepared me for the horror of the photographic session with Andreas. I felt as though I was hurtling on a fast train towards Dante's Ninth Circle, the one where the treacherous are sealed in ice and eternally ripped apart by Satan's teeth. But I'd betrayed Jakey, so I deserved to be ripped apart.

I sat in a little side room in front of a mirror lined with lit bulbs, wearing only an old make-up-stained dressing gown. The wireless claimed it was the hottest day of the year. It was impossibly stuffy in the huge Wimbledon studio Cy Markovitz had hired for the afternoon, but I still couldn't stop shivering. I knew I looked terrible. I had covered my yellowing suntan with dark-brown make-up, but it didn't stop my ribs sticking out like a Belsen victim. I had poured half a bottle of blue drops into my eyes but they were still red-veined and totally without sparkle.

In one corner of the studio, an amazing faggot called Gabriel with very blue eyes and streaked strawberry blond hair, clad only in faded kneelength denim trousers and a snake bracelet, was whisking about supervising two sulky, sweating minions into building a set for me. It consisted of a huge bed with a cane bedhead, silver satin sheets, and a white antique birdcage. One minion kept staggering in with huge potted plants, the other was pinning dark brown patterned Habitat wallpaper to a huge rolled-down screen. Gabriel was arranging a Christopher Wray lamp, a silver teapot and glass paper weights on a bedside table.

'Andreas asked for something really classy to set you off, darling. I've never known him to take so much interest.'

In another corner of the studio to an accompaniment of popping flashbulbs and Ella Fitzgerald on the gramophone, Cy Markovitz was photographing a spectacular looking black girl with 44-20-44 measurements. She was wearing red lace open crotch pants, heels with nine inch spikes, and was writhing against a huge fur rug which was pinned against the wall.

'It's to make her black boobs fall better,' explained Gabriel with a shudder. 'In the pix, it'll look as though she's lying on a bed.'

I turned back to the mirror, sweat already breaking through my newly applied make-up. Then I heard the noise of men laughing; my mouth went dry, my shivering became more violent. Next moment the curtain was pushed aside and Andreas came in reeking of brandy and after-shave, a big cigar sticking out of his mouth. Even heat and drink hadn't brought any flush of pink to his man-tanned cheeks. He was carrying a bottle of Charles Heidsieck and two glasses which he put on the dressing table. I clutched the white dressing gown tighter round me. For a long time he stood behind me looking into the mirror, his eyes as triumphant as they were predatory. Then he said in his oily, sibilant voice,

'You look a bit rough, baby. Been up against it, have you?'

'I've been working hard.'

Andreas laughed.

'You're not cut out for a career, I always warned you. And Gareth Llewellyn's ditched you; I knew he would. You must listen to Uncle Andreas in future.'

He seemed to revel in my utter desperation.

'Never mind,' he went on soothingly. 'I'll see you right. A few weeks of cushy living and you'll soon get the ripe peachy look you had at Grayston.'

He ran his hands over me, lingeringly and feelingly, like a child trying to gauge the contents of a wrapped Christmas present. I gritted my teeth, trying to suppress the shudder of revulsion. He let go of me, and started to take the gold paper off the top of the champagne bottle. I watched his soft white hands in horror. God knows what they wouldn't be doing to me later this evening.

I took a deep breath. 'Can I have the cash now?'

Andreas shook his head. 'Uh-uh. You get the cash when you deliver the goods, and they'd better be good.'

The top shot off the bottle into the rafters. Andreas filled a glass and handed it to me.

'That should relax you,' he said. 'Make you feel nice and sexy.'

I took a belt of champagne, wondering if I was going to throw up.

'Come in boys,' shouted Andreas over the curtain, and we were joined by a couple of Andreas' hood friends, flashing jewellery, sweating in waisted suits. They were the sort of guys who'd give even the Mafia nightmares.

'Meet Mannie and Vic,' said Andreas.

He must have brought them along to show me off. They were obviously disappointed I wasn't as fantastic as Andreas had promised but were too wary of him to show it.

'You wait till she's been with me for a bit,' purred Andreas, pinching my cheek. 'You won't recognize her.'

'Fattening her up for Christmas, are you?' said Mannie, and they all laughed.

Cy Markovitz, having finished with the black girl, wandered over and said he was almost ready. He was a tall, exhausted and melancholy man in his late forties, wearing army trousers, sneakers, and a khaki shirt drenched with sweat.

'Come and meet Octavia,' said Andreas, re-filling my glass. 'She's a bit nervous, first time she's done anything like this, so treat her with care. Lovely isn't she?' he added, smoothing my hair back from my forehead.

Cy Markovitz nodded—he was, after all, being paid vast sums by Andreas—and said the camera would go up in smoke when it saw me.

'You needn't worry about the pix,' he went on. 'We'll shoot through a soft-focus lens with the emphasis on the face and the direct gaze, very subdued and elegant.'

Oh God, what would Gareth say if he ever saw the results. I imagined him suddenly stumbling across them as he flicked through magazines on some foreign news-stand, his face hardening with disapproval, then shrugging his shoulders because he'd always known I was a bad lot. Was it really worth going through with it to help Xander? Was blood really thicker than water?

'Ready when you are darlings,' said Gabriel, popping his golden head round the curtain.

Andreas gave me a big smile. 'Come on baby, you'll enjoy it once we get started.'

I sat on the silver satin sheets, gazing in misery on the forest of potted plants. The studio seemed to be very full of people, all watching me with bored appraising eyes. I huddled even deeper into my dressing gown.

Cy Markovitz came over to me.

'You're not going to need that,' he said gently.

As I took it off, even Markovitz caught his breath. Andreas' thug friends were trying to preserve their poker faces, but their eyes were falling out.

'I told you she was the nearest thing to a Vargas girl you were ever likely to see,' said Andreas smugly.

Cy was gazing into the viewfinder. His assistant took some polaroid pictures, peeling them off like a wet bikini. Andreas and Cy poured over them.

'We'll need the cold blower to stiffen her nipples,' said Cy.

Andreas was determined to get his 112 lbs of flesh. Two agonizing hours later, I had been photographed in every conceivable position and garment, including a white fox fur with a string of pearls hanging over one breast, a soaking wet cheesecloth shirt, black stockings and a suspender belt, and nothing but an ostrich feather.

Gabriel, who was fast losing his cool, had been sent out to hire a Persian cat for me to cuddle, but after 30 seconds of popping flash bulbs the poor creature, having lacerated my stomach with its claws, wriggled out of my clutches and took refuge in the rafters.

Now I was stretched out on the satin sheets, wearing a sort of rucked up camisole top. Cy Markovitz clicked away, keeping up a running commentary.

'Lovely, darling, just pull it down over your right shoulder, look straight into the camera. A bit more wind machine, Gabriel, please. Come on Octavia, baby, relax, and let me have it, shut your eyes, lick your lips and caress yourself.'

'No,' I whispered. 'I won't do that.'

Markovitz sighed, extracted the roll of film from the camera, licked the flap, sealed it up and, taking another roll from the assistant, replaced it.

'Turn over,' he said. 'Bury your face in the sheets, stick your ass in the air, and freeze in that position.'

'I can't freeze when I'm absolutely baking,' I snapped.

'Hold it,' said Markovitz, 'hold it. That's fan-bloody-tastic. Come over and have a look, Andreas.'

Andreas joined him. They conferred in low voices, then Andreas came and sat down on the bed beside me, filling up my glass.

'You're too uptight baby,' he said. 'You're not coming across.'

'How can I when you're all here gawping at me?'

It was like the times when I was a child and my mother insisted on being present when the doctor examined me.

'You'll have to try.' And once again I realized how much he was enjoying my utter humiliation, paying me back for all the times I'd put him down in the past. I lay back on the bed.

'Open your legs a bit further, open wide, that's lovely,' said Cy, clicking away. Any moment he'd ask me to say 'ah'. After this was all over, I supposed I could go out and throw myself over Westminster Bridge.

Gabriel was still whisking about, adjusting plants, his bronzed, hairless pectorals gleaming in the lights.

'Why don't we dress her up as a nun and let Angelica seduce her?' he said. 'Then it wouldn't matter her looking so uptight.'

'That's an interesting thought,' said Andreas.

There was a knock on the door. One of the assistants unlocked it, and let in a girl in a red dress with long black hair, and a pale, witchy, heavily made-up face. She looked furious and vaguely familiar. Perhaps miraculously she was going to take over from me.

'Hi, Angelica,' said Markovitz. 'Go and get your clothes off. We'll take a break for ten minutes.'

'She was on the gatefold of *Penetration* this month,' said one of Gabriel's minions. 'The blurb said Daddy was a regular soldier and that Angelica was reading philosophy at university, and spent the vacation pottering round ruins.'

'You could hardly call Andreas a ruin,' said Gabriel.

Andreas opened another bottle of champagne.

'I've booked a table at Skindles' tonight,' he said, caressing my shoulder with a moist hand. 'I thought in this heat it'd be nice to get out of London.'

He took a powder puff from one of Cy's assistants, and carefully took the shine off my nose. Tears of utter despair stung my eyelids.

'If you could find a horse,' said the other of Gabriel's minions, 'she'd make a stunning Godiva.'

'Shut up,' hissed Gabriel. 'There's a riding school round the corner. I've had enough hassle getting that bloody cat.'

A few minutes later Angelica emerged from behind the curtain, wearing only a red feather boa and a corn plaster. She walked sulkily up to the bed, looking at Andreas with the mixture of terror and loathing such as a lion might regard a sadistic ringmaster.

'You've already met Angelica Burton-Brown, haven't you Octavia?' said Andreas. He seemed to be laughing at some private joke.

'I don't think so,' I began, then realized that she was one of the tarts Andreas had brought down to Grayston. She was now glaring in my direction. Clytemnestra could hardly have looked more blackly on Agamemnon.

'Come and lie down, Angelica,' said Andreas, patting the bed.

She stretched out beside me, her black-lined eyes not quite closed. Underneath each false eyelash was a millimetre of dark venomous light raying straight in my direction. Trust Andreas to set up a scene that tortured both past and intended mistress.

'How's that?' he said to Cy. 'They make a good contrast, don't they? Profane and not-so-Sacred Love.'

I got to my feet and reached under the bed for the dressing gown. 'You've finished with me then?'

Andreas put a heavy hand on my shoulder, pressing me down again.

'On the contrary,' he said, 'we're only just beginning. Put the Nun's headdress on Angelica,' he said to Gabriel.

She looked so utterly ridiculous—talk about sour Angelica—that I was hard put not to giggle with hysterical laughter. But not for long; the next moment Andreas had hung a cross round

173

my neck.

'Kneel beside her, Angelica,' he went on. 'That's right, as close as you can.'

I felt as though great toads were crawling all over me. I gazed down at the cross hanging between my breasts. Perhaps if I held it up to Andreas, he would suddenly age hundreds of years and shrivel into dust like Count Dracula.

'Now put your hand on Octavia's shoulder,' he said. I jumped away as I felt her fingers.

'No!' I screamed. 'No! I won't do it, I won't!'

'Cut it out,' said Andreas. 'Do you want two grand or not?'

I looked at him mutinously; then I remembered Xander and nodded.

Angelica looked about as cheerful as a cat with toothache. She'd obviously never had bread like that from him.

Andreas ruffled the sheets round us, and gazed into the view-finder.

'Very nice,' he said softly. 'A bit more amiable, both of you.' Cy took over again.

'Put your hand on Octavia's throat, Angelica,' he said.

I steeled myself, feeling the tense hatred in her fingers. The sweat was glistening on her black moustache.

'Lovely,' said Cy. 'Now slide your hand down a bit Angelica, and down a bit further.'

I couldn't bear it, even for Xander, I couldn't take any more. I shot a despairing supplicating glance at Andreas and was appalled by the expression of suppressed excitement on his face. I felt the tears coursing down my cheeks.

Then suddenly there was a tremendous crash outside. Every-one jumped, as someone started pummelling on the door.

'It's the fuzz,' squeaked Gabriel in excitement, patting his curls.

'You can't go in there,' screamed a female voice. 'The studio's booked.'

'Oh yes I bloody can,' shouted a voice.

There was another tremendous crash, the door seemed to tremble, then suddenly caved in. I gave a gasp, half of relief and half of horror, for in the doorway, fierce as ten furies, terrible as hell, stood Gareth. Slowly he looked round the room, taking in first Cy, then Andreas and his hood cronies, then finally me on the bed with Angelica. With a whimper I pulled one of the satin sheets round me.

'What the bloody hell's going on?' he howled, walking across the studio towards me. 'You whore, you bloody cheap whore! I might have known you'd end up like this. Get your clothes on.'

Andreas moved towards him.

'Take it easy, big boy,' he said softly. 'Don't get so excited.'

Gareth turned on him.

'You lousy creep,' he hissed. 'I know how long you've been scheming to get your dirty hands on her. I'll get you for this. Go on,' he added, out of the corner of his mouth, to me. 'For Christ's sake, get dressed.'

I stood up, still too frightened to move.

'How on earth did you know she was here?' asked Gabriel, looking at him with admiration.

'Andreas shouldn't go round boasting in restaurants,' said Gareth. 'These things get overheard.'

'Look, wise guy.' Andreas was talking slowly and patiently now, as though he was dictating to an inexperienced secretary. 'You're gatecrashing a very important party. Cy's booked for the day, and so's Octavia, and neither of them for peanuts. She needs the money, don't you Octavia?'

Gareth glanced in my direction. I nodded miserably.

'So you can't come barging in here making a nuisance of yourself,' said Andreas.

'Oh, can't I?' said Gareth with ominous quiet.

There was a long pause; then, suddenly, he went berserk. Turning, he kicked Cy's camera across the room, then he smashed his fist into Cy's face, sending him flying after the camera. The next moment he'd laid out Cy's assistant with a punishing upper cut. Then Vic the hood picked up a rubber plant and hurled it at Gareth, who ducked just in time and, gathering up another plant hurled it back.

Screaming like a stuck pig, still in the Nun's headdress, Angelica dived under the bed, followed immediately by the two minions and Gabriel.

'Oh dear,' sighed Gabriel as two more plants sailed through the air. 'Burnham Wood came to Dunsinane, now its going back again.'

Ducking to avoid more flying vegetation, I shook off the silk sheets, ran across the room, dived behind the curtain and started to pull on my clothes. By the sound of it Gareth was still laying about him like a maddened bull. As I looked out he was having a punch-up with Mannie who wrong-footed him and sent him crashing to the ground. The next moment Gareth had got to his feet and thrown Mannie into the middle of the remaining potted plants.

'Oh my poor jardiniere,' wailed Gabriel's voice from under the bed. 'What *will* the plant shop say?'

As I crept out from behind the curtain, a silver teapot and two glass paperweights flew across the room, none of them fortunately hitting their target.

Gareth paused; he was breathing heavily. Cy was still nursing his jaw in the corner. Mannie was peering out of the plants like a spy in L'Attaque. Vic was shaking his head and picking himself up. Cy's assistant got to his feet. As he started edging nervously towards the door, Gareth grabbed him by the collar.

'No you don't,' he said. 'Where are those rolls of film? Come on or I'll beat you to a pulp.' His fingers closed round the boy's neck.

'Over there on the trolley,' choked the boy in terror.

Gareth pocketed the rolls. As I sidled round the wall towards him, he glanced in my direction and jerked his head towards the door. He was just backing towards it himself when Vic moved in, catching him off guard with a blow to the right eye. Gareth slugged him back, sending him hurtling across the room, then, trying to right himself, tripped over one of the light wires and cannoned heavily into a pile of tripods. It was getting more like Tom and Jerry every minute.

Next minute, Andreas, who'd been watching the whole proceedings without lifting a finger, picked up the champagne bottle and, cracking it on the underneath of the bed, moved with incredible speed across the room towards Gareth. Cornered, Gareth scrambled out of the tripods, shaking his head. His right eye was beginning to close up. His forehead, just above his eyebrow, was bleeding where Vic's gold ring had gashed it.

He backed away from Andreas until he reached the wall.

'Now then big boy,' murmured Andreas, his voice almost a caress. 'I'll teach you to get tough with me.' He brandished the jagged edge of the bottle in Gareth's face. 'Give me back that film.'

Gareth stared at him, not a muscle moving in his face.

'You lousy cheap punk,' he said.

Then I froze with horror as I saw that Mannie had extracted himself from the potted plants and, armed with a flick knife, was moving relentlessly in from the right. Without thinking, I picked up the Christopher Wray lamp and hurled it at him, slap on target. Just for a second Andreas' concentration flickered, giving Gareth the chance to leap on him, knocking him to the floor. Over and over they rolled like Tommy Brook and Mr. Tod, yelling abuse at each other. Then finally Gareth was on top smashing his fists into Andreas' head. For a minute I thought he was going to kill him; then he got up, picked Andreas up and threw him through the Habitat wallpaper like a clown through a hoop.

There was another long pause. Gareth looked slowly round the room. Everyone flattened themselves against the wall or the floor. Then suddenly there was the sound of clapping, and Angelica emerged from under the bed, her Nun's headdress askew.

'I've been waiting three years for someone to do that,' she said.

Blood was pouring from Gareth's arm. He must have jagged it on Andreas' bottle.

'You'll bleed to death,' I moaned, gathering up a peach silk petticoat that was lying on the floor.

'Well, bags I give him the kiss of life,' said a little voice from under the bed. Gareth grabbed my wrist. 'Come on, let's get out of here.'

19

I hoped Gareth had worked off his rage breaking up Cy's studio, but as we stormed up Parkside towards London, with Wimbledon Common on our right, the full storm of his fury broke over me.

'I tried to help you,' he yelled. 'We all did. Jakey's nursed you like a baby through the last eight weeks, and then you have to pick this afternoon to blow the whole thing—just when Jakey needed you. I don't understand you, Octavia. Have you got some sort of death wish? Don't you care about anyone?'

He overtook another car; you could have got fag paper between them. Thank God we were going against the traffic. Home-going commuters crawling in the other direction stared at us in amazement. Some of them were stopping to put their hoods up. The stifling heat hadn't let up, but an ominous, bilberry dark sky had replaced the serene unclouded blue of the morning.

'Why did you do it?' said Gareth, overtaking yet again. 'Go on, I want to know.'

'I can't tell you.'

'Sure you can't. Well I'll tell you; you're so bloody idle you can't resist making a quick buck from Andreas. But my God, you'd have paid for it. He'd have broken you in a couple of months.'

We were passing Wimbledon Windmill now. I gazed stonily at the dried-up pond and the great sweeps of platinum-bleached grass, blackened everywhere by fires.

Gareth warmed to his subject:

'I guess you're turned on at the thought of all those men on news-stands slobbering over your photograph, misting up windows in Soho to get a second glance at your tits, not to mention the ones in bedsitters wearing raincoats . . .'

'They'd hardly keep their macs on in the bedroom,' I protested.

'Don't be flippant,' he howled.

We had reached the roundabout at Tibbet's Corner now, but he was so incensed he kept missing the turning off to Putney and had to go round three times, which didn't improve his temper.

'Don't you give a fuck about your reputation?'

'I don't care,' I snapped. 'I needed the bread in a hurry, that was all. But you're so well-heeled you wouldn't understand things like that.'

Gareth turned on me, enraged.

'Haven't you any idea how poor we were when I was a child?'

'I don't want to hear,' I said, putting my hands over my ears. 'I've read D. H. Lawrence, I know quite enough already about poverty at the pithead. I'm just fed up with you going round censoring my behaviour. Who the hell do you think you are, Mary Whitehouse, you great Welsh prude?'

'You've called me that already,' he said.

'What!' I shouted, my hands still over my ears.

'Don't bug me,' he shouted back and, seizing my arm, yanked my hand away from my ear.

I sat very still, watching the white marks left by his fingers slowly turning red. Then out of the corner of my eye I noticed the peach silk petticoat I'd tied round his arm completely drenched in blood, and a red stain creeping down his blue check shirt. He'd gone very white. Suddenly the fight went out of me.

'For God's sake let's call a truce and go to Roehampton

Hospital. You need stitches in that arm,' I said.

'I don't want any stitches,' he said, screeching to a halt at the top of my road. Leaning across, he opened the door.

'Now get out, or I'll throw you out, and don't come grovelling back to Jakey either. You're on your own from now on.'

And, swinging the car round, he drove off in a cloud of dust.

As soon as he'd gone I began to shake again. How the hell was I going to tell Xander I hadn't got the money? I hadn't got the rent either. Mrs. Lonsdale-Taylor was sure to sling me out. The trauma of the afternoon had left me in a state of total shock. Numbly I walked towards the river, kicking my shoes off, when I came to the Common, not even noticing the sharp dry grass cutting into my feet.

A large drop of rain fell on the path in front of me. Perhaps at last the drought was at an end. The poplar trees by the bowling green clattered their leaves in a sudden gust of wind. The light was curious, as though one was swimming under water. Picnickers and dog-walkers hurried home, looking anxiously up at the sky; even the rooks were silent. The river bank was covered with coke tins, bottles and old ice-cream cartons. Two dogs were splashing about in the water, cooling off. I wished I had Monkey for company.

A large drop of warm rain splashed on my face, then on my hand; the discoloured sky was suddenly veined by lightning, followed three seconds later by an earth-shattering clap of thunder. The whole valley seemed to be boiling, the rain was coming down faster now, pattering on the leaves above me, pitting the river with rings, bouncing off the iron-hard ground. Another flash of lightning unzipped the sky, followed by another, far more brilliant, which seemed to snake down the centre of a huge elm tree only fifty yards away, and rip it apart. Then the whole sky exploded with rain.

I didn't care. I wanted to be struck down. I put back my head, feeling the drops dripping down my neck, cascading on my face, washing away all the horrible stage make-up. In two minutes I was drenched. The lightning was coming at the same time as the thunder-claps now; it sounded like Gareth up in heaven breaking up another studio.

I don't know how many hours I wandered round, half crazy with grief. I felt like Lear: 'poor naked wretches, whereso'er you are, that bide the pelting of this pitiless storm.'

Then suddenly it was getting dark, and the storm was moving away, grumbling like a drunk turned out of the pub. The rain was letting up, night was falling. In the distance I could see the orange lights on the roads around the common. It must be nearly ten o'clock.

Xander, Mrs. Lonsdale-Taylor and the music had to be faced. Listlessly I started to walk home. I was frozen and drenched. The temperature had probably dropped to the seventies, but after weeks up in the nineties, it felt like mid-winter. My pink smock, worn on Andreas' instructions, had instructions of its own on the label about being only dry-cleaned. Wet-cleaned, it had shrunk drastically, risen to mini-skirt level, and was now clinging to every inch of my body. My hair was hanging in dripping tendrils. People giving their dogs last runs before bedtime looked at me strangely as I wandered barefoot past them. The whole common was steaming now like a crocodile swamp.

I walked listlessly up the street, the drenched gardens bowed down under their great weight of water. The gutters ran like millstreams, the street lamps reflected in the wet pavement. I paused outside my digs, trying to screw up enough courage to go in, rubbing the rain from my eyelashes. The iron gate was ice-cold beneath my touch.

The next minute Monkey hurtled out of the front door and threw himself on me, yelping hysterically, licking my hands, scrabbling at my bare legs with his claws. I tried to creep up the stairs past Mrs. Lonsdale-Taylor, but she shot out of the kitchen, her tough roast beef face rigid with disapproval.

'Damn storm's snapped off half the delphiniums,' she said.

'Oh, I'm sorry. What a shame, after the way you've nursed them through the drought,' I said, sidling up the stairs, but she was not to be deflected.

'Where on earth have you been? Your office has been ringing

all day. People have been calling in. You're not in any trouble are you? I hope you've remembered the rent.'

'I'll get it by tomorrow.' I had reached the bend in the stairs now.

'The agreement was every fourth Friday in the month,' she called after me, 'so I'd like it now; and there's someone waiting for you upstairs. I told you I won't have men in after nine o'clock. He must go at once.'

With a heavy heart I climbed the next flight. It must be Xander, waiting for the cash. I opened the door. The room was in darkness. Then my heart gave a lurch. A man was standing against the window. No one could mistake the width of those shoulders. It was Gareth.

'What are you doing here?' I whispered.

'Looking for you,' he said.

'I don't understand.'

'I love you,' he said simply, 'and I can't go on anymore.'

I ran towards him: 'Oh please, hold me.'

He put his arms round me and, as he kissed me, I felt the strength and warmth and love flowing out of him.

'Oh darling,' he muttered into my hair. 'Christ, I'm sorry. I was so angry this afternoon, but I was so jealous and I didn't understand what was going on.'

'I couldn't help it,' I said, starting to sob hysterically. 'It was the only way I could get the cash.'

'I know it was. Hush, sweetheart, hush. I've been with Xander since I left you. I was so miserable, I had to talk to someone. He told me everything.'

'Oh God, what's he going to do?'

'He told Pamela, then he went to the Police. It was the only hope. I took him to the station and held his hand for the first half hour. He'll be all right.'

'But what did Pamela say, and Ricky?'

'Darling, I really couldn't care less.'

'I couldn't let Xander down,' I muttered. 'He's always looked after me.'

'I know, I know, you're a bloody star, I just wish you'd come to me, instead of Andreas. Now for God's sake get out of those wet clothes.'

He let go of me and switched on the light. My legs wouldn't hold me up any longer so I sat down on the bed, gazing dumbly at him. His right eye had closed up completely now. He was still wearing the same blood-stained shirt but at least someone had bandaged up his arm. The next moment he'd pulled my suitcase down from the top of the wardrobe and, taking my dresses off the hangers, started throwing them in.

'What are you doing?'

'Packing. You're getting out of here.'

'I haven't got anywhere else to go,' I whispered.

'You're coming home with me.'

'But I can't. Lorna wouldn't like it.'

'What's she got to do with it?' He picked up my cornflower blue dress. 'You were wearing that the first time I met you. Put it on now.' He put it on the bed.

'But you and Lorna,' I was gagging on the words. 'Aren't you going to get married?'

He stopped for a second, his hands full of my underwear.

'What on earth gave you that idea?'

'She did. She said, you and she.'

'Not *me, Charlie!*'

'Charlie,' I said stupidly. '*Charlie!* But how on earth?'

'They met at your place,' said Gareth. 'The night she stayed with you, he asked her to come along to the shop, started taking her out, and bingo. She said you said you were crazy about someone that night. She assumed it was Charlie. That's why she felt so awful about telling you.'

'Oh God,' I said. 'It was you all the time. I never stopped loving you for a moment since that evening I was sick on the boat. God, what a stupid muddle!' And I started to laugh, but it went wrong in the middle and I started to cry again. Gareth chucked the rest of my underclothes into the suitcase and put his arms round me, holding me so tight I thought my ribs would crack.

'Now for Heaven's sake get that dress off or I'll strip it off you myself.'

I started to blush. 'I can't while you're looking.'

He grinned. 'After that matinée earlier, I can't see much point in false modesty.'

Then he must have seen something in my face because he turned his back and started talking to Monkey who was sitting shivering in the suitcase.

I'd just peeled off my wet smock when there was a loud knocking on the door. I grabbed a towel as Mrs. Lonsdale-Taylor walked in.

'Miss Brennen,' she spluttered. 'I've told you I won't have men in my house. You must leave at once,' she added to Gareth.

'She'll be out of here in five minutes,' said Gareth curtly, 'so beat it.'

'Don't you dare address me like that, young man,' said Mrs. Lonsdale-Taylor. 'What about my rent? She owes me £60.'

Gareth put his hand in his pocket and pulled out a wad of notes. He counted out six tenners and gave them to her. Then he looked at poor little Monkey still shuddering in the suitcase.

'How much d'you want for the dog?'

'He's not for sale. He belonged to my late husband.'

'Ten quid,' said Gareth.

'Well, it doesn't seem right.'

'Twenty,' said Gareth, thrusting the notes into her hand. 'Now get out, you fat bitch, and bully someone your own size.'

Three quarters of an hour later, Gareth and his two waifs had reached home, and were sitting in the drawing-room. Although I was wearing one of his sweaters and nursing a large glass of brandy, I was assailed once again by a terrible fit of shaking. The tension was unbearable. The only sound was Monkey gnawing ecstatically on the remains of a leg of mutton which Gareth had found him in the fridge.

'He's happy,' said Gareth. 'Now it's my turn, come here.'

'I can't,' I said in a stifled voice.

'All right, I'll come to you.'

He sat down on the sofa about a foot away from me. I gazed

desperately at my brandy.

'I'm now going to give you a short lecture,' he said. 'If you had any idea what I've been through since we got back from the boat, wanting you so fucking badly I thought I'd go up in smoke. I know I showed it in a funny way, fighting it because I didn't want to betray myself, because I couldn't see any way that you could possibly feel the same way about me. The reason I finally agreed to take over Seaford-Brennen was because it gave me a chance to keep in touch with you, and that wasn't the only length I went to, sucking up to your degenerate brother, Xander, in the hope he might put in a good word for me, ringing Jakey every evening to see you were O.K. Why do you suppose none of the guys there ever laid a finger on you? Because I'd have fired them if they had.'

'I don't b-believe you,' I said incredulously.

'Don't interrupt,' he said. 'You're also right about my being a Welsh prude. I couldn't stand anyone coming near you. I nearly went spare over Jeremy and Charlie. This afternoon, as you saw, I flipped my lid.'

'You were wonderful,' I breathed, putting a hand up to touch his poor bruised eye.

He grinned, imprisoning my hand against his cheek:

'There's something to be said for being brought up in the valley. Then I talked to Xander. He told me about your childhood, and your parents and what a lousy deal you had all along. But that's all over now.'

And, kneeling beside me, he took me in his arms. I started to cry.

'What's the matter?' he whispered.

'It's no good,' I sobbed. 'I love you more than anything else in the world. I'm crucified with longing for you, but that's just in my heart. You were right from the beginning, I am frigid. I've been to bed with so many men I can hardly remember, but I hated it with all of them. I can put on a good act, but inside I just freeze up.'

'Hush lovie, hush.' He was stroking me in that soothing way you might gentle a horse.

'I'm telling you this because I love you, I'm no good to you.'

'I'm the best judge of that,' he said. 'You've never been properly loved in your life, just spoilt, and told to push off and play somewhere else, and produced to show off when grown-ups came to tea because you're so beautiful. Come on,' he went on, pulling me to my feet and leading me towards the bedroom. 'Let's not muck about any more.'

'No.' I shrank away from him. 'You'd be disappointed. I couldn't fake it with you.'

'I won't, because I don't expect anything. We've got to get used to each other.'

In the bedroom he switched on a sidelight, illuminating the vast double bed, and drew back the fur counterpane. As he undressed me with undeniable deftness, I thought of all the women he must have laid on that bed before me . . . I felt like a novice horse entering the Horse of the Year Show for the first time, with the jumps up to six feet and all the previous competitors having had clear rounds.

Once we were in bed he just held me very gently until the horrors of the day began to recede. Then he said:

'I'm not going to lay a finger on you tonight. You're too tired.'

I felt a stab of disappointment.

'At least I don't think I am,' he went on, putting a warm hand on my tits, spanning both nipples with finger and thumb.

'Look,' he whispered, 'I can stretch an Octavia.'

I giggled.

'That's better. Come on lovely, remember, from now on I've got custody, care *and* control of you—and I'm not going to leave you, like your bloody mother did, ever again.'

And with infinite tenderness he kissed me, until I felt the waves of lust begin to ripple through me.

'It's Friday,' he said, as his hand edged downwards. 'We've got the whole weekend ahead. We needn't get up at all.'

Then later he said, 'Relax sweetheart, don't try so hard, there's no hurry. I actually *like* doing these things for you.'

Then later, more harshly, 'Stop fighting me; we're on the same side.'

Then suddenly it happened—like a great, glorious, whooshing washing machine—it's the only way I can describe it—leaving me shuddering and shuddering with pleasure at the end, like the last gasps of the spin-dryer. And afterwards I cried some more because I was so happy, and he held me in his arms, telling me how much he loved me until I fell asleep.

A few hours later the dawn woke me. We'd forgotten to draw the curtains. All I could see were huge windows framing the plane trees of Holland Park. I blinked, turned and found Gareth looking at me. I must be dreaming.

I put my hand out to touch his cheek.

'Are you real?' I said incredulously.

He smiled. 'I am if you are.'

His eye had turned black, his chest was covered in bruises.

'I think I'm in bed with Henry Cooper,' I said. 'I never dreamt he'd make such a sensational lover. Do you think we could possibly do it again?'

And we did, and it was even better than the last time, and I screamed with delight and joy because I'd been so clever.

When I woke again he wasn't there. I looked round in panic; then I found a note pinned to the pillow.

'Gone shopping with Monkey. Back about eleven. I love you, G.'

Still overwhelmed with wonder at what was happening to me, I got up, wrapped myself in a towel and, wandering into the kitchen, found a pile of unopened mail. I flipped through it. Three envelopes were written in distinctively female hands. I turned them over. One was from someone called Michelle in France, another from a Sally in the Middle East, another hadn't put her name on the back, but it was post-marked Taunton, and she'd written 'private and confidential' on the bottom.

I stood, overwhelmed with terror. Gareth had had millions of women before me. What was to stop him having millions in the future? Last night's protestations might have been just a ruse to get me into bed. I couldn't bear it. I went back into the bedroom and sat shaking on the bed, feeling myself pulled down into the familiar black slimy cavern of horror.

'Keep calm,' I kept saying to myself. 'It's all right.'

Suddenly I jumped out of my skin as the telephone rang. It was Mrs. Smith.

'He's not here,' I said. I could feel myself bristling.

'Well that's all right. Just give him a message that everything's O.K.'

'I'll tell him,' I said stiffly.

Mrs. Smith laughed, 'I'm so glad you two have finally got it together,' she said. 'He's been absolutely insufferable since he came back from that boat trip. It'll be nice working for a human being again.'

'Oh,' I stammered, feeling myself blushing all over. 'Do you mean to say—was it that obvious?'

'Yes,' she said. 'He's a very dear man. I think you're very lucky, and if you look behind the drawing-room door you might find something else to convince you.'

She dropped the receiver.

I ran to the drawing-room. Behind the door were two canvases stacked against the wall. I turned them over and gave a gasp of delight. One was my Adam and Eve picture, the other the Cotman. I looked at them incredulously, tears filling my eyes.

Then I heard a key in the door, and a scampering of feet. Monkey, rushing up the stairs, reached me first, but the next moment I was in Gareth's arms, with Monkey frolicking and frisking round our feet.

'I was worried some of Andreas' hoods might have got you. Annabel Smith says you've been like a bear with a sore head since the boat trip,' I gabbled incoherently. 'And you bought back my pictures; it's the nicest thing anyone's ever done for me, I can't believe it. When did you do it?' I added as we went upstairs.

'Last week sometime. I didn't hang them. I thought you could decide where you want to put them. But I'm not having Adam and Eve over the bed to distract you whenever we have sex.'

I went scarlet. 'I suppose bloody Xander told you that.'

He stopped in the doorway of the kitchen and kissed me on my bare shoulder.

'Christ, you're beautiful Octavia. Do you feel you can really put up with a jumped-up Welsh gorilla for the rest of your life?'

Then he kissed me on the mouth.

'Xander ought to be shot,' I said when I could speak, blushing even more furiously.

He laughed. 'I'm only teasing you.'

The telephone rang. 'If that's Mrs. Smith again, she said you weren't to worry about anything,' I said.

It was Xander.

Gareth listened for a minute; then he said, 'That's great. Talk to Octavia.'

'Hullo darling,' said Xander. He sounded very cheerful.

'Are you all right?' I said.

'Well things have been pretty heavy. Ricky made the most awful scene, and I hoped very much Joan was going to have a coronary, but Pammie was staunchness personified; she told them both to get stuffed. And the police have pulled in that little snake, Guido, so all in all things haven't turned out too badly. And I must tell you,' he lowered his voice, 'I do fall on my feet. There is the most enchanting constable in the C.I.D. here who's been too marvellous to me.'

'Xander, you are *awful.*'

'Well since you've taken Gareth away, I had to find some compensation. Look, I'm terribly sorry, I'd no idea you'd have to take your clothes off to get me that money.'

Gareth was frying bacon and eggs when I came off the telephone. Stroking Monkey, I told him about the police constable.

'He's quite incorrigible,' said Gareth. 'All the same he'll be nice as a brother-in-law.'

My hand stopped in mid-stroke.

Gareth turned the bacon thoughtfully, then he shot a sideways glance in my direction.

'What did you say?' I whispered.

'I said I was looking forward to having him as a brother-in-law.'

'You shouldn't tease,' I stammered.

'I'm not teasing. I told you I'd been shopping this morning.'

He extracted a dark blue leather box from his pocket, his hand shook slightly as he handed it to me. So did mine as I opened it. I had terrible trouble with the clasp. Inside was the biggest sapphire I'd ever seen.

'Oh,' I breathed, 'is it really for me?'

'No one else.' He switched off the bacon and slid it onto my finger.

'W-what about your harem of girls, Annabel Smith and co?'

'I'll give them up if you will.'

'You don't *have* to marry me,' I said.

'Oh yes I do,' he said. 'I'm not a Welsh prude for nothing. I want to regularize things, particularly for Monkey, make him feel more secure.'

I giggled.

'I'm going to put my mark on you, so no one else can get near you,' he went on, his eyes suddenly serious. 'But I warn you, baby, even if we have to fight like cats, I'm going to wear the trousers. You're going to do what I tell you, and if you start upstaging me, I'll put you down. The boys in the Valley are like that. We keep our women in the background and we beat them if they give us any trouble, but we know how to love them.'

Suddenly I felt my knees giving way with lust.

'Could we possibly do it again just very quickly before breakfast?' I asked.

We never made it to the bedroom, but the kitchen floor proved perfectly satisfactory.

THE END

APPASSIONATA by JILLY COOPER

They called her l'Appassionata, though her real name was Abigail Rosen. She was the sexiest and most flamboyant violinist on the music scene, adored by her fans and lusted after by every man who watched her play. She was also the loneliest and most exploited girl in the world. When a dramatic suicide attempt destroyed her career as a violinist, she was determined to conquer the conductor's rostrum.

When Abby was given the chance to take over the Rutminster Symphony Orchestra she was ecstatic, not knowing that the RSO was in hock up to its neck and was composed of the wildest bunch of musicians ever to blow a horn or caress a fiddle. Doing her best to pull her undisciplined rabble into something resembling an orchestra and at the same time trying to pretend she was not *wildly* attracted to Viking, the fatally glamorous French hornplayer who claimed *droit de seigneur* over any pretty woman who joined the orchestra, stretched Abby to near breaking point. It wasn't helped when the new managing director of the RSO proved to be a rough and rugged Yorkshireman who decided that what the RSO needed was some tough discipline. And then Rannaldini came on the scene with Machiavellian plans of his own to wreck the RSO.

The effervescent champagne of Jilly Cooper's new novel takes us into the magical, funny, wildly rampageous world of the classical orchestra. All her sparkling and outrageous characters are back – Rupert and Taggie Campbell-Black, Hermione, Boris Levitsky, Rannaldini – in the most sexy, delicious, and heart-warming novel of the year.

NOW AVAILABLE AS A BANTAM PRESS HARDBACK

0 593 03863 0

OTHER JILLY COOPER TITLES
AVAILABLE FROM CORGI BOOKS
AND BANTAM PRESS

THE PRICES SHOWN BELOW WERE CORRECT AT THE TIME OF GOING TO PRESS. HOWEVER TRANSWORLD PUBLISHERS RESERVE THE RIGHT TO SHOW NEW RETAIL PRICES ON COVERS WHICH MAY DIFFER FROM THOSE PREVIOUSLY ADVERTISED IN THE TEXT OR ELSEWHERE.

☐	13895 9	**The Man Who Made Husbands Jealous**	£5.99
☐	13552 6	**Polo**	£6.99
☐	13264 0	**Rivals**	£5.99
☐	14103 8	**Riders**	£6.99
☐	11149 X	**Imogen**	£3.99
☐	10878 2	**Prudence**	£3.99
☐	10576 7	**Harriet**	£3.99
☐	10427 2	**Bella**	£3.99
☐	10277 6	**Emily**	£3.99
☐	10241 3	**Lisa & Co.**	£4.99
☐	03863 0	**Appassionata (Hardback)**	£16.99

All Transworld titles are available by post from:

Book Service By Post, PO Box 29, Douglas, Isle of Man IM99 1BQ

Credit cards accepted. Please telephone 01624 675137, Fax 01624 670923 or Internet http://www.bookpost.co.uk for details.

Please allow £0.75 per book for post and packing UK.
Overseas customers allow £1 per book for post and packing.